Beginnings of a Dream

Beginnings of a Dream

Zachariah Rapola

Some of the stories in this collection have appeared previously in the following publications:

Mayibuye, Tribute, Botsotso, Imprint, Staffrider, Running Towards Us – New Writing from South Africa, Unity in Flight, Oprud, Post Traumatic, and *Words Gone Too Soon.*

First published by Jacana Media (Pty) Ltd in 2007

10 Orange Street
Sunnyside
Auckland Park 2092
South Africa
+2711 628 3200
www.jacana.co.za

© Zachariah Rapola, 2007

All rights reserved.

ISBN 978-1-77009-210-5

Cover design by Michiel Botha
Set in Bembo 10/12pt
Printed by CTP Book Printers, Cape Town
Job No. 000281

See a complete list of Jacana titles at www.jacana.co.za

CONTENTS

Introduction	ix
Prologue	xv
Beginnings of a Dream	1
Fragments of a Dream	31
Rituals for Martha	45
Last Parade at Golgotha	61
Street Features	73
Death and the Palmist (*Letter from the dead*)	85
A Soothsayer's Deposit	105
When a Name Awakes	121
Arunah's Jigsaw Puzzle	133
Alley-Alley, Where is My Lover?	143
Lesiba the Calligrapher	155
Epilogue	*179*

DEDICATION

I dedicate this book to my late father
for being generous enough to sow the
dream before leaving.

Agee! Motau, robala o nabe maoto.
Re ka se tsoge re go lebatse, wena ga
mmogo le ba bina Tau ka moka ba
robetsego.

Hle! Le se re furalle, re thekgeng, re feng
matla le bohlale bosego le mosegare
ge re kalokana le go hemahemitshwa ke tsa
lefase la ka keno.

A salute also to my former mentors,
Professor Ezekia Mphahlele,
Nadine Gordimer and the late
Lionel Abrahams for nurturing and tending
to the dream to maturity.

INTRODUCTION

Gobane lefatshe ruri le humile ka marapo a bahu gammogo le digahla tša marapo a bona le phušuphušu yeo bogologolong e bego e le marapo a bona.

For the earth is rich with the bones of the dead, as well as the remains of their bones and the powder which in the past used to be their bones.

– O K Matsepe

With *Beginnings of a Dream,* Zachariah Rapola takes the reader into a phantasmagoric world where streets are paved with human remains, men are apocalyptically condemned to death by the fire of their loins, Indian goddesses are reincarnated as young women who never menstruate and can't stop playing with jigsaw puzzles, and children are the issue of botched abortions; virgins can no longer be found in the villages, the wisdom of elders is ridiculed, and those who commit suicide are unable to counter the weight of tradition. And yet, despite recurrent nightmares, the world is also home to calligraphers, who continue to record dreams that encompass the past, present, and future in a sort of Borgesian circularity.

In 'Street Features', Rapola personifies a street in downtown Johannesburg. Everything happens on it: couples mate, children fly kites, drunkards brawl, sex workers stroll, pickpockets steal, the homeless seek refuge. It is a bewitched path; a snake is said to breathe beneath the street. The narrative voice observes the changes the street undergoes over a period of ten years and remarks on how the street witnesses people's lives from childhood to old age, on how many battered souls leave the city for the rural areas. Palesa, a prostitute and 'a weaver of words', captures the narrator's attention, but after he becomes infatuated with the woman he is unable to disentangle her from the structure of the place. So she becomes a 'street feature', just like the narrator himself: forever embedded in its sediments. With a foreboding of endless repetition, Rapola endows the street with human qualities while depicting the indissoluble union between the urban space and people: the street as witness, flat dwellers as the foodstuff of its existence.

The absolute certitude that life begins in dream, that the world beyond is what lends ours a semblance of reality, and that only the mediation of ancestors offers a link to the gods – this has seldom been expressed with the depth of conviction one finds in this collection. In the title story, a grandmother is prevented from dying until her namesake is born to her youngest daughter; in 'Fragments of a Dream', the celibate main character suffers not one but three deaths; in 'Death of a Palmist (*Letter from the Dead*)', a deceased sibling posts letters from the underworld; and in 'Lesiba the Calligrapher', the most anguished dream is one where the ability to dream is lost.

While Bloke Modisane infused life into the disappearing rubble of Sophiatown in *Blame Me on History*, K Sello Duiker diverted our gaze from Table Mountain towards the troubling shadows it casts in *Thirteen Cents*, and Phaswane Mpe embodied the metamorphosis of Johannesburg's inner city in *Welcome to Our Hillbrow*, Rapola is the chronicler of contemporary Alexandra: 'a giant sea of darkness that feeds on remnants of frightened life'.

Beginnings of a Dream bursts the seams of a township gone haywire. Through surrealist imagery and a haunting poetic force, we are exposed to the glare of social collapse; we see the sores apartheid left in the people who most painfully experienced it, and for which the post-apartheid dispensation has, as yet, not offered redress. The burden is heaviest on children who are the prey of rapists, on girls driven to clandestine abortions, on ageing women who have lost the place of honour traditional society once granted them, on young men turned into alcoholics by the affliction of AIDS. At the same time, the viciousness of place (which reflects a vicious history punctuated by forced removals, overcrowding, poverty and unemployment) is humanised through Rapola's fiction. Township 'gangland' territory contains also the mischievous grins of toddlers, the fear of mothers, the bravado of young boys. 'Gangland' is a word that conjures up hard-core images, a hard, man's world. People's faces, their eyes, get lost in the term. Rapola's writing, in stories such as 'Rituals for Martha', 'Last Parade at Golgotha' and 'Arunah's Jigsaw Puzzle', cuts through the hardness and lets us appreciate from within the fears of young boys and girls growing up in that environment, life being short and brutal – and all the other truisms that pervade conversations in Alexandra and beyond.

This collection reflects Rapola's relationship to English as it fuses with his mother tongue and with colloquial South Africanisms. In some cases, one cannot say whether the story was originally written in English or Sepedi. And this carries with it a linguistic sedimentation that helps re-invent current South African literary life; in these stories, the movement from one language to another occurs seamlessly. It is a narrative suffused with the reality of linguistic pluralism that young South African writers enjoy today. The translated Pedi proverbs, rather than distracting from plot, provide links to the cultural and literary traditions Rapola is tapping. More visible, or perhaps just more immediately recognisable to a westernised reader, may be the Christian ethos traversing the collection, as well as the appearance of Greco-Roman mythological figures.

Zachariah Rapola figures prominently among a new generation of South African writers whose fiction brings to life the literary *zeitgeist* of their continent. And yet, for all its contemporary relevance and vibe, *Beginnings of a Dream* has at its core a dialogue between the living and the ancestors that creates a powerful resonance between the bones of the dead and the echoes of their survivors.

Isabel Balseiro
Alexander and Adelaide Hixon Professor
of Humanities
Harvey Mudd College
Claremont, California, USA

PROLOGUE

DREAMERS

dreamers have come & gone

long before the dawn of capital
long before the tide of servitude
dreamers have come & gone

peasant dreamers of long & fugitive
dreams

i have shared in their longings
when bound & shackled skies mocked
their wandering thoughts
peasant dreamers of long & fugitive
dreams

dreamers here & gone

a nomad
nourished on intuition i weaved through
their desires

dreamers here & gone

i have cried & longed too
when they dream of oceans & winds

for i too am a dreamer
a dreamer
of long & fugitive dreams

BEGINNINGS OF A DREAM

Birth is the beginning of a dream
a meditative pose over knights and queens
on the tightrope,
a juggle of divining bones
striving to interpret man's prodigal wanderings
through the Minotaur's labyrinth…

BIRTH IS THE BEGINNING OF A DREAM… In my old age, I am able to muse. My grandchildren dismiss my observations as senile rattling – and how can I chastise them for their ignorance, when even my four adult children push aside my accumulated insights as 'grandmother's tales'? Perhaps they are right, how can I tell? Increasingly, my thoughts are becoming blurred by dust and drifting winds.

I overheard Thekiso, my sixteen-year-old grandson, whisper to Itumeleng, his ten-year-old sister: 'Hai! Tsamaya, go keep grandmother company. Can't you see she is desperate for an audience?'

Desperate for an audience! This is how the insights of my old age are viewed. Trivialised and trampled upon. Dismissed as bothersome.

Maybe Thekiso is right. I know I am constantly talking to them – when they are doing their homework; when they are trying to enjoy their favourite television and radio programmes. In regard to interrupting their homework, I too feel I might be intruding. But I cannot agree with them when it comes to the other things. For, in my long years, I have learnt a lot. I have accumulated knowledge and information, and discovered that these two instruments, radio and television, offer nothing good. The parables and wisdom that age has nurtured in my head are lacking in them, as are the revelations and inner resourcefulness that rains and winds have nourished in me. Increasingly, with the advance of age, I realise that these appliances are contraptions designed to curb the growth of inner knowledge.

Innocent grandchildren, how can I chastise them? Their innocence and ignorance is the mandatory price of youth.

It is Raisibe whom I cannot forgive. Raisibe, my first-born. I could have excused her were she a boy, for then there might have been a wife whom

I could blame instead, since it is true that wives are experts at souring relations between mother and son. The worst was when she called me a witch. That was seven years ago. I wonder how that husband of hers copes?

Birth is the beginning of a dream... and a fragment of that epic dream exploded into a nightmare in 1980. That is when Madika died. At sixty-eight, I found myself a widow. Maybe because we had got so used to each other, the two of us had started believing in our immortality. Not that death didn't visit us; it was just that we were too stubborn to host him. We were prepared to sink into the grave together, so that we might walk side by side in the hereafter. It is now almost twelve years since Madika's death. And here I am, alone. Still, I am grateful for my luck. Few people can withstand the assaults of old age as I have. I have also given up counting the white hairs on my head. And you wonder whether I am grateful or not – of course I am. But here I am, all alone in this shadeless world. Occasionally, I venture outdoors. But a hostile world always sends me scuttling back into the familiar comfort of the house. My ears can no longer wander out to visit different sounds or voices. My eyes, too, no longer can sprint about, entering the sealed windows of other homes. Only my voice strolls around the house. Still, my children and grandchildren, like everyone around me, at times erect walls around their ears. 'Oh grandmother, *please...*' In my old age, when the word 'please' should be pleasing to hear, it is now like a needle that pierces the core of my heart. I blame Raisibe for that. Raisibe is the worst. On her occasional visits, she uses the standard: 'Oh grandmother, *please* – you've had your breakfast / lunch / supper / snuff... what more do you want?'

As if I live only for food and snuff. As if I were not her mother. She surely treats me like her stepmother – one of those frowned-upon fleas that drain the blood bond between fathers and their children.

That is why I feel betrayed by Madika. His sneaking away to the beyond without taking me. Had death made his advances to me instead, I certainly would have informed Madika, and invited him to come along – even dragged him.

'Hai! Tsamaya, go keep your grandmother company...'

Thekiso has changed a lot. He has changed for the worse. It must be that mother of his who is putting bad things into his head. I remember how attached the boy was to me. That was until he turned eleven. Then he discovered the bioscope. He stopped brewing grandmother's favourite coffee; stopped boiling grandmother's Maltabella porridge. He didn't care any more to bring her warm milk after supper. I spent hours contemplating these disappointments, and concluded that old age was a curse.

Looking after my grandchildren is my greatest pride. Caressing their innocent little faces used to thrill me. Mother! Foundation rock of the family. Like the baobab tree, sustaining life throughout the centuries; stretching out her firm hands to protect her children, like the bark of the baobab protects its roots so they don't get bruised when drawing water. And Madika is looking after our children and grandchildren from the beyond – the world of the ancestors.

I know I will join him. All the meandering footpaths in this world lead to death. One day I will escape from this lonely life… this bondage of old age.

Old age contains a curse, the curse of extreme loneliness. During the years of supervising the birth of my grandchildren, I was always looking for the arrival of my other self, a granddaughter who would bear my name, thus ensuring my resurrection. I had seen her in my many visits to the other world, when dreams transported me to the beyond. On the left side of her forehead, immediately below the hairline, there would be a tiny pink spot. A red thread-like line would cut from her left collarbone down to her navel. After the birth of each girl, I would strain my eyes trying to identify these features. But each birth followed the last without the new arrival sporting these marks. Then I knew the waiting was going to be long. But it was a wait worth all my patience, for I knew the birth would signal my time to depart to join Madika.

Of late, he had been visiting me frequently, to give assurances that such a child would come. Still, I was sceptical. Wasn't he the same person who reneged on our promise to depart together? His visits, though, served to confirm another thing – the level of my perception. My eyes, in surrendering my journeys of discovery in this world, were now attuned to seeing the inviting doors to the other world.

Sleep is temporary death; Madika told me this on one visit. For nights after that, I awaited his arrival. But he did not reappear. Later, I was to learn that his non-appearances were a protest against my quarrel with Raisibe. They are attached, those two. I understand. Raisibe was our first child. Her birth had a great impact on Madika's life. Already in his late thirties, he was a notorious skirt-chaser. I could sense his fear of not fathering a child. That was clear from the varied aphrodisiacs he drank before making love. I recall one time he brought home a litre bottle of bull's urine. Days later, in a hidden plastic container, I saw a stallion's testicles. Then I saw him eating them raw. Eventually he started accusing me of being barren. Meanwhile, his skirt-chasing continued unabated.

It was only when he started chasing fourteen- and fifteen-year-olds that I became alarmed. Then he said to me: 'Wena! Your parents should bring back half the amount of my lobola. So much for a wombless thing, e-ehee!'

But Raisibe came, and Madika relaxed.

During his life, Madika favoured Raisibe. This attachment had to do with Madika's restored confidence in his virility. This close bond between father and daughter was viewed suspiciously, for in our village fathers were supposed to be closer to their sons. Also, I suspect our other children were jealous, since they tended to tease her about everything.

Madika's repeated assurances that my other self would come filled me with pleasure; but there was also that uneasy feeling that I was waiting for my vanquisher. For though she was to issue from my daughter's loins, it was only by usurping my life that she would be able to carry on with hers.

My life and hers were intertwined like those of larva and butterfly, where the former must undergo complete transformation for the other to appear. Or I was like a snake, that must shed its worn skin to renew itself.

Would this girl, my replica, uphold the dignity and virtue which I had maintained throughout my life? Kana! Girls these days like competing with men. As if our ancestors were foolish to make them female.

Why couldn't it be a boy? Boys never become rivals to their grandmothers. How I wished for a little boy. And I realised that, in old age, I had fewer and fewer wishes.

My last quarrel with Raisibe took place after one of those rare good suppers she is capable of cooking. As I knew, things between her and Modise were bad. It was as if she had made the meal to infuriate him, for it was said that good food was bad for tempers in his family. A pig is their totem; a pig is known to relish filth. So was it true that anything above filthiness raised Modise's ire?

As a son-in-law, he was not my favourite. I was only grateful that he had relieved me of a bad-tempered daughter – and, to a lesser degree, that he'd saved us from having a spinster in the family.

Shame, poor Tidimalo, my sweet younger daughter. She and her husband, Tshepo, hardly visited us. I understood. Their life was more settled. Two sweet things, they were like twins. Peaceful creatures who take after their names: Tshepo, trusty and reliable, and Tidimalo, quiet and withdrawn. But Raisibe and Modise... joo badimo!

I was quietly talking to my grandchildren. Sharing with them the wisdom old age had helped me accumulate. Modise, that hopeless horse-betting addict, was absorbed in his TAB calculations, while Raisibe was busy with her ironing. What was it that stopped her? Maybe it was Thabang's insistence that he would never again go to sleep. I remember that just before he said this,

I had said something like: 'Yes, children of my child, we too as children used to hear of it from our elders. Of course we never believed it. Until two days ago...'

At which Thabang exclaimed, in the innocent high-pitched voice of little boys his age, 'Two days ago! Nkgono, what happened?'

'Your grandfather told me...'

'Told you! How could he tell you? Dead people don't talk.' That was Mmabotle, my nine-year-old granddaughter. That one should have been named Tidimalo, after her aunt, who in her quiet way always insisted on finding answers. Her mother complained that she was dull. But I knew, and it filled me with grandmotherly pride to see this bright girl. With time I knew she would open up, absorb the sun and radiate. She was destined to be the exception in a family where daughters did not excel, despite the naughtiness they displayed when young.

'They do talk, my little one – they talk to us during night visits that seem like dreams. Or at times it is we who cross over to their land.'

'How come I sometimes dream of the stove and wardrobe chasing or fighting me, but I don't cross over anywhere?' That was Thabang.

'Yes my child, we all do. We all do in our dreams. For sleep is temporary death, where the worlds of the living and dead merge into one...'

'Ooo! Grandmother please, stop telling those children nonsense. I know it is because of that good food you ate.'

Was that talk from Raisibe, my own daughter! 'What! Am I a pig?'

'Yes! Grandmother, you are. Hoji ka mphela.'

'Yes-yes, go on – I am one because you bewitched me.'

'Howoo! What about you old people who refuse to die – killing young people so you can sustain your lives on theirs?'

At this point, Modise picked up the children and disappeared with them to the bedrooms. Finally he came and dragged Raisibe away.

Within me a voice kept repeating, 'Damn your cursed good food.' I was having great difficulty in breathing... and then suddenly everything stopped.

When I awoke, I was in a strange country. Birds, bees and flowers, all radiant despite the fog that was drifting about. All my deceased relatives were there, feasting in a welcoming ceremony. Except Madika. 'Where is he?' I kept on asking. I was finally told that he would not appear until

I had gone back to make peace with Raisibe. I started to look for her, but she was nowhere. I looked everywhere. And I was moving further and further away from the assembled relatives.

I returned to consciousness alone in my house. It took a while to forget the insult of my own daughter calling me a witch. After that, it was difficult for us to relate. I heard she had forbidden her children to visit me. Modise was the only one who did come by occasionally. He kept those visits secret from Raisibe – as I knew by a strange dream I had. In my dream, I saw a mourning Raisibe in a strange forest. She was wandering about in circles like a dog sniffing for the lost spoor of a hare. Then Modise and I appeared to her. When she saw us she turned into a python, which started its death-dance, preparing itself to strike. When Modise charged forward to face it, it changed back into Raisibe. And she fled from him, despite his vowing not to do her any harm.

When I asked him about her and my grandchildren on his next visit, Modise responded by weeping. That confirmed another suspicion of mine – that whenever my name was mentioned before her, Raisibe responded with tears.

After a year of us not seeing each other, I finally resolved to go and visit her. I thought it right that I not tell anybody about this visit. I quietly wrapped myself in my green and white mjajana and off I set.

I arrived at her house at noon. I was hesitant to step onto the dirty front stoep. I could see she was still busy cleaning. I stood for a while, not daring to venture across the accumulated dust that all households manufacture at night. For who knows, among those bits and pieces of dirt might be a pin or granule dropped by witches the previous night, with a spell cast on it to cause a stroke in anybody who might tramp on it. I did not trust Raisibe.

When I entered the kitchen door, she stared at me like someone seeing an apparition. She started sliding backwards, her arms raised protectively to her chest. And I knew what was happening, and started laughing.

'Hela ngwana tena. Tlaa! Daytime is a blanket which the dead cannot wrap themselves with. Come. It's me – your mother.'

That broke her trance. She shrieked, gasped, 'Mme! Mme!' and ran into my arms. It reminded me of years gone by, when she was still a little girl, always seeking my arms for reassurance and comfort.

'Mme! How did you manage...?'

'I walked, my child.'

'Walked! But Mme... why? You should have asked Modise to drive you.'

'Huwii, you spoiled children! Even now you don't appreciate the saying of our ancestors, that no elephant has ever complained of its trunk as a burden.'

'Oo Mme dear... grandmother of my children. What can I do...?'

'Nothing, my child. The moon cradles her burden, and has never asked the sun for help.'

'Mme... I feel so bad. Forgive me...'

I knew she was going to embark on a confession, which I wasn't eager to hear. In tearing the entrails of that long-dead animal, we were bound to pierce the gall bladder. 'Aowa Raisibe. The sun's rays have dried the skin, clearing the foul smell as well. Let us not like ungrateful hunters go back searching for maggots to plant on it.'

She hastily baked fatcakes and then made tea. We sat drinking and eyeing each other like orphans, separated in childhood, who have managed to trace each other.

'Eya! Mme, your grandchildren are still at school.'

'How is Thabang? The naughty one. You should take him to Ga-Mamahlola. The boy should learn to herd and milk cows.'

'Haa! Nkgono, is there time for cows and goats these days?'

'You should have seen my own herd. I had twelve calves, twenty cattle – no... five – five – five... about twenty-five cattle.'

'Mme, when was that? Because you said you came to Ferndale in fifty-nine.'

'Yes, that was the year red ants descended on us.'

I think it was this talk of the old days that helped heal the rift. It reminded me again of when she was young. She would always pester me to tell her more. Sometimes my memory would fail me, and then I would invent events. She enjoyed them all the same.

The children came back from school. At first they skirted around us, not sure whether to come and embrace Nkgono or not. Thabang was the first to approach me. 'Nkgono, yesterday I again dreamt of the wardrobe,' he said. 'It stole my toys. Then it joined Mmabotle in beating me...'

'O-maka!' That was Mmabotle.

'Ke nnete,' Thabang insisted. 'See, Nkgono.

You see this scratch. It was caused by both with the brown belt.'

'Thabang, you didn't show me that,' Raisibe said, edging forward.

'She said she would buy me sweets at school if I don't tell.'

'Joo! Maka. A makana?' said Mmabotle. 'Such big lies.'

'It's true, Nkgono. I'm telling because she never bought the sweets.'

Bana ba ngwanaka… that pride of seeing my grandchildren came again. Soon they would be man and woman, raising their own children.

Modise arrived. Like the children, he was at first unsure of how to relate to me, but soon joined in the happy reunion. They wanted to buy a frozen chicken, but I insisted they buy a live one. We made an offering to the ancestors with its blood. After that, we had a ritual supper. Thabang grumbled at being denied the opportunity to crush the bones, but we explained that those would be offered to the ancestors. Afterwards, Modise drove me home.

That night, as expected, Madika appeared to me. I smiled as he went about crushing chicken bones with relish. I couldn't resist bursting into laughter when he started licking his fingers and choking.

'Eehee! Rakgolo-a-bana, don't shame me,' I said. 'You mean I haven't been feeding you?'

'Eya, mosadi. You were too busy with your quarrels. Look, my nicely nourished belly is gone.'

'Aowa, Rakgolo-a-bana. You sit about with your arms folded, your hunting spear rusting – and you complain of hunger.'

'Mosadi, you remember how much I paid for lobola...'

'Eshee! What was three pounds, after all? Youngsters of today will shame you. Utlwa! Our neighbour's son paid six thousand last month. That excludes expenses he will bear for presents to his in-laws. And you boast of your pittance.'

'Maka! Listen to me... I want two goats. Phoko le tshadi – a billy- and a she-goat, wa ultwa!'

I again burst into laughter: 'Why the billy? You mean you still want to be the stud?'

'Mosadi! You!... So you knew all along about me.'

We both laughed. In the morning when I awoke, my ribs were still aching from that laughter.

Three days later, on Saturday, I called a family meeting. I prepared mageu, thopi, mala le mogodu and samp porridge. Tidimalo and Tshepo came in their new car. Those two are going places, I tell you. Raisibe and Modise came with their children. A few of our other children came as well.

'Bana-ka, taba ke ye; your father says he is starving,' I told them. 'I teased him about it, but you know what will happen if you ignore him.'

'Mme, what should we do?' Hau, Raisibe, asking such a stupid question.

'Mme, I think we should slaughter a cow.' That was Tshepo, the pride of any mother-in-law.

'Aowa, bana-ka. Your father explicitly said he wants a male and a female goat.'

'Look, Mme, if he is really starving as he says, then a cow would be appropriate. He'll feast on bigger chunks. What do you think, Modise?' That was Raisibe again.

'Hmm! Not that, child. Give the ancestors what they want. Not what you think is good for them. Your father said two goats. And it should be that.'

'I agree, Mme,' said Modise. 'Let us respect his preference.'

And so it was settled.

Of course, Madika had his reasons for his demand. That I know. But I couldn't tell them. I couldn't tell them that he had said he was lonely and missed me terribly. That it was time I considered joining him. He had confided in me that the billy's virility would finally help sire the awaited infant. He also said that Tidimalo would be the passage through which that infant would come.

'But Rrakgolo-a-bo, you have always said Raisibe would be the bearer,' I had challenged him.

'I did not come to argue, but to deliver a message,' was his response. His instructions were that Tidimalo's name be chanted when the billy was slaughtered. She was also to eat the she-goat's womb.

'No-no,' she said when I told her all this. 'That I don't like. I am not barren.' It was understandable. No woman likes that kind of insult.

'Aowa! Tidimalo, nobody said that,' I soothed her.

'Then why, why should I be the one chosen to eat the she-goat's womb? Why? I guess my husband will be expected to eat the billy's testicles as well. Hee! Isn't that so? Tell me, Mme, is it wrong if we prefer to have children later? Look, you think my womb is tied. No-no, I prevent.'

'Whaaat? Tidimalo! Why, you too... you too use those things?'

'What things, Mme?'

'Don't they use dead people's ovaries and such things, ijoo! Ke ya go tshaba ngwang tena.' I looked at her in shock. 'Tidimalo! I thought you were a sensible and responsible girl.'

I spent a long time trying to convince Tidimalo to do as requested. Tshepo was also sceptical. They finally asked to be given time to think the matter over.

A week later, a sobbing Tidimalo phoned me. 'It's Raisibe, Mme...'

'What about her?'

'She said it serves us right for disregarding the ancestors.'

'Ngwanaka, what is this all about?'

'Tshepo's new car was dented from behind... and... I phoned Raisibe... and Mme, she said it is just the beginning. My own sister talking like that. I know she has always been jealous of me and Tshepo...'

'Maybe you didn't hear her properly...'

'No Mme, I did. I could hear the suppressed laughter in her voice.'

'And how is Tshepo?'

'He is okay, Mme. Only he is becoming nervous.'

'Nonsense, man, Tidi. Why should he? Accidents happen everyday. Not to trees or stones, but to people…'

'But Mme, the day before, his cheque book and credit cards were lost. He said it was as if they simply disappeared. He too is starting to suspect that something terrible will happen.'

'Ngwanaka, your father and our ancestors are not evil people. Why this terrible conclusion then?'

After the telephone call, I offered a silent prayer to our ancestors. I also resolved to discuss the matter with Madika that night.

When it was already past one o'clock and sleep had not come, I became worried. I slipped out of bed, took my snuff pouch, sprinkled some snuff on the floor and invited him to visit me. Sleep followed immediately.

'Why do you disturb my peace?' he demanded as soon as he appeared.

'Ga go bjalo papa. The coop is broken into, and I am worried that the mongoose might steal the newly hatched chickens. Rra-bo, your children are panicking. Why, tell me, are you offended?'

'You wake me from my sleep for that?'

'Rra-bo, don't brew a storm where there is none. Tidimalo and Tshepo believe you are punishing them...'

'A bird does not build a nest so as to destroy it later. Ga go bjalo, mma-go bana. Tell the children not to worry. Tell them my only worries are occasional hunger and loneliness.'

After that he disappeared. I tried to call him back, but he refused to come again. Then I knew my time to join him was a wink away.

Age is a time of withering, a battle with worldly storms. I came to that conclusion through toil and pain. I realised that childhood was a blessing. I could no longer understand what was happening around me. It was a shock for me to see little children argue with or insult adults.

Later, I saw them running around in the streets carrying placards with slogans: *Forward with Children's Rights... Down with Capital Punishment... Freedom Now, Education Later.* What nonsense was all that! I knew a child's freedom consisted in having enough to eat before going to sleep and on waking up. Children at meetings telling their parents how they should be treated... what nonsense. It became clear then why old people hasten to the grave. To avoid witnessing all this humiliation.

In my case, I decided to withdraw into myself. I found solace in talking to myself. My ignorant grandchildren labelled it 'old-age mumblings'. It was all due to my desperation to depart this damned world.

At last, Tidimalo and Tshepo relieved me. 'Mama, nna le Tshepo, we have decided to go ahead... isn't that so, Tshepo?'

'Eya, Mama. We think for our sake and yours we should partake in the ancestor-appeasing ceremony.'

I looked at them proudly. Sweet things. 'A badimo ba le thogonolofatse.'

Four weeks later, on a Sunday morning, we performed the ritual. Tidimalo and Tshepo's only concern was that none of the other relatives should know that they were to eat the animals' testicles and womb. How could I deny them that request?

Thereafter, it looked as if a well-fed Madika was dispensing largesse. My monthly pension was increased. Then: 'Mahlogonolo! Tshepo has been promoted at work.' That was Tidimalo's phone call a couple of weeks later.

'We've done it, Mme! We've done it!' That was Raisibe.

'What... what is it Ngwanaka?' I asked.

She laughed, cried and kept on clapping her hands. 'Yooooo! Mme, Modise got the Pick 6... he got fifteen thousand!'

But Tidimalo, on hearing of Tshepo and Raisibe's good fortune, complained, 'But Mme, that money rightly belongs to us. I mean, if we had refused to eat those things during the ceremony, they wouldn't have got that money.'

'What talk is that now, Tidi. Don't be jealous.'

'I'm not. How could I be – those low-class people, so many children...?'

'Tidimalo! What has got into you?'

'Mme, it's just that I find it unfair. Tshepo and I partake in the ritual... then those two get such a lot of money...'

The call left me shivering with shock. Tidimalo – I had always thought she was rational and mature. It dawned on me that I didn't really know my children as well as I'd thought I did.

A few months later, Tidimalo called again to inform me that she was pregnant. I knew my time for celebration had come. I stocked up on wool and cloth and started knitting and sewing for my granddaughter.

'But Mme, shouldn't you wait first?' Tidimalo asked. 'What if it is a boy?'

'Tidi, I know what I am doing.'

'You know, Mme, distant fountains cannot be relied upon.'

'Eshee! What do you know? For fifty years I relied on my dreams to place bets with the Chinaman. And every time I got him.'

Tidimalo reached her ninth month. As instructed by Madika, we performed another ancestor-appeasing ceremony. Raisibe refused to attend the ceremony. The reason she gave was that Tidimalo had insulted her and Modise – referring to them as 'that starving, flea-infested lot' that her generosity had rescued. Also, Tidimalo made the habit of reminding them that she had eaten the goat's womb.

That night, after the ceremony, I waited for Madika to come. But he did not show up. Instead, his late sister, the one our Raisibe is named after, came. She informed me that the insult directed at Raisibe was an insult to herself and Madika. The next day I asked Tidimalo to apologise to Raisibe. She refused.

The expected birth pains arrived. And I braced myself to be the first to see that infant. When thirty-six hours had elapsed without the child coming out, we realised something was wrong.

Tidimalo was rushed to hospital. After examining her, doctors pronounced her fit to go through a normal birth – though it proved otherwise.

With worry, Tidimalo kept asking me, 'Mme, is my child "tied"?'

'No. Such delays do happen.'

'Why then, why is it refusing to come? Tell me, Mme, who is refusing its entry into this world?'

I took snuff, home-brewed mageu and beer, and made an offering to the ancestors. That night, the aunt came to me. And again stressed that until the insult directed at her namesake, Raisibe, was withdrawn, the child would never come out.

Innocent Tidi – how would she take that rebuke?

'Why? Why should I apologise? Isn't it true that they are poor? How many times have I and Tshepo saved them by lending them money? Everybody knows that throughout his life, father favoured Raisibe. The only inheritance he left her was being spoiled. I won't, Mme, I won't apologise.'

'Aowa! Tidi, you know the consequences. Always remember: don't interfere with those whom the ancestors turn to with a warm smile, lest they direct the cold hand against you.'

My words eventually persuaded her. She went to Raisibe and apologised.

Madika came that night. He was beaming in triumph. Yet this time I knew I had to admonish him. 'Rra-go bana, what is all this? Are you short of better games to play?'

'Mosadi! Ga ke batle selo ka nyakea Raisibe, kwaa! I swear, woman – Raisibe is don't-touch.'

'Isn't Tidimalo your child as well, hee? Is a simple apology worth a human life?'

'Thaetsa faa! Your sister-in-law says she is tired of cooking for me. You must make haste over to this side.'

'Listen, Rra-gwe, I was never lazy or scared of the pots during our life together. What's all this talk about now?' Men! As if I was lingering merely to avoiding providing him with a square meal every day.

One morning a couple of days later, as I was sweeping my stoep, I slipped and fell. I awoke with a cast on my right leg. Shame! What did I think would happen, at my age? And the doctors said I would have to spend a week in hospital.

It was during that time of my confinement in hospital that I received the message that Tidimalo had given birth.

'When? Is it a girl? How does she look? What

is on her forehead and collarbone?... Go fetch the child... take me to her, now-now!'

'She is beautiful, Mme,' said Tshepo.

'Where is she? I want to see her. Her forehead and collarbone... what did you see there?'

'Please, Mme, relax. Your granddaughter is fine. You will see her when you are able to walk...'

'What! I want to see her now! Go fetch her.'

Finally the baby was brought to me. Those little eyes, unseeing still, responded to me. All the foretold birthmarks were there. I turned to Tidimalo. 'It is her, everything about her. It is a pity, my child, she will never enjoy the privilege of being nursed by her grandmother.'

'What do you mean, Mme? You know we won't take her to any crèche.'

'I know, Tidi. There are bones galore, yet the dogs have lost their teeth; I no longer have the strength to bear her on my back or rock her on my lap.' Unlike Thekiso, Itumeleng, Thabang or Mmabotle, she would never enjoy my tender care.

'And Tidi, who are you going to name her after?'

'Mme... Tshepo and I haven't decided everything yet. She will at least be called Mmogedi.

Of course among her names she will have your name, Molatedi, as well.'

'How did she respond… when you gave her my name?'

'She gurgled with joy.'

'Yes, she should, she should… my faithful one… grandmother's own mother.'

Extreme fatigue then took hold of me. I knew I needed sleep.

Sleep is the beginning of consummation. A blanket which all wrap themselves in, offering comfort to all, widows, orphans and the poor. I know my sleep will be a well-earned one. I will awake again when the world starts making sense to my little other self.

Old age is the winter of disintegration. Or season of hibernation and renewal…

FRAGMENTS OF A DREAM

Cyprian was a sickly boy. He grew up to become a lonely young man. When I first met him, he was still in the habit of wetting his bed. He was twenty-three then. But you shouldn't mistake him for abnormal. He was sane, in his own way. At times he even appeared old, like the emaciated, young-old men of Biafra. There were times, at night, when I saw something like a phosphorescent halo around him. Maybe it was my imagination. There were also times during the day when he would appear embalmed in a haunting paleness – again, maybe that was my imagination. It was in this context that I came to know Cyprian more closely. We became friends. Even our friendship was strange. I myself was twenty.

'You are a funny girl,' my mother used to say.

And of course she was right. Then, girls of my age were not supposed to be tomboys. At my age, I was supposed to be being groomed for marriage. I was strange. When I did eventually start to experience normal urges, I was desperate to find some impressive attachment, before it was too late.

And Cyprian was there. He was sick, but there was always an aura around him. So my insignificance found solace in his patronage. With time, I would come to model my fantasies about men on Cyprian. While to many people his passage on this earth was light and feathery, to me he was the exact opposite. There were times when, in my sleep, I could hear the tremors of the earth caused by his vibrant footsteps.

And yet his manhood couldn't make a tremor. Because Cyprian couldn't kiss. Neither could he make love.

'Do you masturbate, then?' I asked him one evening, as we stood by a dead 'Apollo' lamp-post.

'No, I don't,' was his response.

I looked deep in his eyes, which reflected only calm and innocence.

'Do you do other men, then?' I jabbed.

To this he responded that he didn't know how.

'You are certainly sick… you must see a doctor, or a sangoma,' I told him. My eyes scanned him from his feet up. At the same time, a strange tingling shiver crept all over me. There and then I knew I was in love.

'I am in love… in love with a sick man.' The words kept spurting from deep within my consciousness. My attempts to stifle them were futile.

'You are sick!' my mother would yell at me, years later. 'It is because of that sick boy of yours.'

This was after I had confided in her about the strange feelings that by then had become familiar to me. Whenever I reached an orgasm when making love to my husband, Cyprian would appear. Sometimes he would just watch me accusingly. But then there were times when he would become violent. He would grab Dikapeso, my husband, and shove him aside. Then he would mount and ride me to unimaginable ecstasy. Perhaps my mother was right about me being sick. How else could one explain those incidents? For Cyprian had been dead then for eight years.

I remember when he died. He told me that on that night he was awakened by a commotion outside his room. He said he heard blaring police sirens and tiptoed to his window to look. He flipped back his curtains slightly, but then a gust tossed them wide open and flung his window open at the same time. There was a giant searchlight trained on him. He noticed a platoon of uniformed men, all with sniffer dogs, and marksmen ready to storm his room. He recognised them as members of the well-known and feared counter-insurgency unit. A blaring loudhailer commanded him and his accomplices to come out with their hands raised. Laden with terror and confusion, he dragged himself to the door.

The scene outside was even more terrifying. A squadron of six Alpha XH1 helicopters was hovering above. Further on, surrounding his yard, was a division of Ratel-90s, their hungry turrets zeroed in on his one-roomed house. When he hesitantly descended the four steps to the ground, a pack of sniffer dogs hurled themselves at him.

But no. That was not the day he actually died. In fact he was to die six years later.

My affair with Cyprian was passionate but non-erotic. We were lovers before all except ourselves. For I could not reach him. I could not arouse him – because he had other desires. And it was only on his death-bed, in hospital, that he opened his heart's secret to me.

Throughout that ordeal, he implored me to remain with him. It was now my turn to comfort his traumatised soul. That was also to be the first and last time he kissed me. I well remember that kiss, for it left an imprint on my lips.

And then Cyprian told me about his relationship with another woman. For many hours I listened, and became familiar with my rival. I kept quiet. There were times I thought he would fall silent from sheer exhaustion. But he went on and on. She was thirty-three... she lived alone... she was still a virgin... they were in love, and were planning to marry some day... she stayed at Nineteenth Avenue, near the Jukskei River... she was the perfect, prettiest, most innocent woman...

But then he contradicted himself. He explained that his bed-wetting was a result of his erotic couplings with her.

I was suddenly jerked to full alertness when he told me she was there in the room.

He introduced us and made teasing comments. 'I swear, Mmabatho,' he said to me, 'should you once again postpone our wedding, I am going to take off with this angel.' His face radiated a waxy glow of contentment. His eyes would now and then fix on me, then stare back at her.

I knew something was wrong. Either I was dreaming, imagining things or plainly mad... or else he was. For there was nobody except the two of us in the room. After his long monologue, a period of silence followed. It was only when he had ceased breathing that I saw, or thought I saw, two shadowy figures clinging to each other as they left the room. In that misty apparition I could well make out his tall and bony profile, and the silhouette of a beautiful woman.

It seem to me that he had finally died.

I jumped up from his bedside and uttered a hollow, prolonged shriek – quite unlike my normal, restrained self. It was a strange, hideous scream.

'She's mad! She's mad.'

'Get her, man, get her – strap her on the bed.' A stampede of nurses and orderlies came after me.

My mother later told me that I'd brayed like a donkey. And years later, she said that the same sort of sound was repeated when I gave birth to my quadruplets.

But not exactly... for Cyprian did not die that day either. In fact, it was another three years before he really did die.

One day, out of nowhere, just when I was longing for some romantic sweet-talk from him, he said: 'From tomorrow, I start with my hunger strike.'

'Why do you want to go on a hunger strike?' I asked.

'I want to know my origins.'

'But that is ridiculous – how can a hunger strike, or fast or whatever you call it, help you in that?'

He seemed to think deeply, then said: 'I don't have a father or mother; still, I'm no fool. I want to know why I was born in such circumstances, and the only source left to reveal that to me is nature.'

'Look, Cyprian, I do understand your situation...'

'No, you don't.'

'Okay, maybe I don't. I'm just trying to understand.'

'No, no! You certainly do not, and never will!'

'But Cyprian, I am your friend, your lover!'

'No, you are not. And stop pretending you are.'

I stood there, humiliated and stunned by that explicit rejection. Yet there was no malice in his eyes. I struggled to remain calm, but finally gave in. I felt the veins in my soul bleed, and finally the fibre of my composure burst. A stream spilled from my eyes as that fragile inner river turned into tears: sour, salty and bitter they were. Trickles that neither my palms nor handkerchief could restrain. Nothing except his gentle touch and hesitant, comforting whispers.

His response triggered a memory of a conversation I'd once overheard between a decorated Koevoet veteran and a conscientious objector. The two were debating the moral rightness or wrongness of hunger strikes for political convictions, as compared to fasting for spiritual redemption. After hours of arguing, the two ended in tense silence – then chuckled, laughed and finally embraced in fraternal solidarity, because they realised that logic and rationality were merely transient states of the mind. The war veteran was still a passionate humanist at heart, while the pacifist was still a maniac, only temporarily strutting in robes of peace to pacify his troubled conscience. During one of his previous lives, he had butchered his fiancée.

Cyprian argued that a fast cleanses the bowels. 'This simple ritual enables man to communicate with greater powers and to fulfil his potential, which overloaded bowels deny him.' He was convinced that the ritual, as he preferred to call his hunger strike, has the same effect as baptism – to purify. Psychopaths, paedophiles and other rogues would only have to go on a fast to redeem their sins, while monks, nuns and pacifists could embark on hunger strikes to purge the occasional lust and temptation.

After this revelation he became restful; his eyes stopped wandering about, jabbing at space for answers. 'A sad soul like mine was not meant to be tortured by such an existence... my only regret is that I am going to leave you behind.'

'What about Squiza?' I teased him, referring to my rival. 'Aren't you taking her along?'

'I doubt she will agree. You know, after four years of dating, she hasn't yet made up her mind about a lesser commitment like marriage...'

'Cyprian, you are really extreme. You consider marriage a lesser commitment. For me, for us simpler people, it is the ultimate factor in life.'

'Then what I would like her to do is to walk with me for the last mile of the journey. Just wait and see...'

Cyprian's voice was to keep on echoing in my mind. 'Damn fool!' I sighed. This boy was certainly sick. Now I believed my mother.

I did wait and see. And what I saw wasn't pleasing. From that time, I began to know and understand. But all the sympathy I offered him was not sufficient to cushion him against the knowledge that was to come, nor the renewed torrent of emotions it would precipitate. After that day, I could never again face him without feeling ashamed. Though he never said it, I knew also that I represented shame to him. At times I thought it was contempt. He had made his most damning revelation, and I was the only witness.

For a long time, we tried to downplay the inhumanity we represented to each other. For Cyprian was male, and I was female. Two beings who were now exposed in our nakedness. For in truth we were executioners – wild, heartless beasts feeding on each other. Our passion was an epitaph, a hollow oratory peddled as a serenade. A love song we both diligently sang while with lustful glee we sharpened axes to terminate each other's lives – the eternally estranged twins.

I could see his large, wandering, depressed eyes. Struggling to understand his life, his existence. But there was no one to give him hints or provide him with answers… until his haunted quest stumbled upon the truth. And that made him swallow his heart. For Cyprian was conceived after the rape of his girl-mother by her child-boyfriend's friend. And to erase and escape the shame, she'd gone for an abortion. All of that was mirrored in his eyes: the dingy, filthy, smelly, inhospitable 'operating theatre'.

Doesn't it make sense now? His insisting I wouldn't understand him. Of course I could never have understood that his dreams would forever be blemished by endless harrowing screams and pools of blood. A nightmarish sacrifice that he miraculously survived – and yet finally succumbed to. Could he always then, even in me, his beloved, have been seeing those phantoms – predatory monsters masquerading as human beings?

That scenario when soldiers came for him was yet another episode of an epic nightmare. Those soldiers were toys or puppets, manipulated to perform another scene in a million-act play. The play was a tragedy, starting with the Chief of Counter-insurgency dreaming of a holed-up band of operatives at 324 Nineteenth Avenue. It climaxed with the storming of Cyprian's room, and ended in a flop when only rats and mice were found there, screeching. But because the tragedy's appetite could not be satisfied, it chose to extend its tragic grip until Cyprian's will to live gave in.

In the end, I could only sigh in guarded relief. Because it was a self-defeating nightmare. A death long dead before its birth. An apparition whose attempt at haunting brings only mild irritation. For Cyprian, as I knew him, or as I would have liked to have known him, was long dead. He quietly died on that fateful night in a darkened alley when he was conceived. He was yet again to die, on that rainy day in a dark mkhukhu when he was hastily expelled from his mother's womb. Though he survived, the darkness of the alley and the mkhukhu were forever stamped on his forehead. In the end, he disappeared into the multitude of the condemned, into the giant sea of darkness that feeds on the remnants of frightened life in what is called Alexandra.

The elegy in its unravelling became complex. For the odds were stacked against him. How was he to be normal when all elements that shaped his existence were abnormal? His veins, his whole being was contaminated with spiteful semen. That organ, swelled with greed and rage and vengeance. With those pictures and thoughts crystallising, I started choking and throwing up...

It has been ten years since Cyprian's death. The passage of time seems to have tamed his jealousy, as he appears less and less during my love-making sessions with Dikapeso. But nostalgically, I still remember my Cyprian. I agree, I am a happily married woman with four children. But what can I tell my boys and girls? They are still babies. I wish that they could grow up to adulthood and die still being babies at heart. Knowing nothing. Immune from life's realities. I am also happy that Cyprian never lived to see them.

Out of respect for our love, I named one of my children Cyprian. Both my husband and his parents opposed the move, arguing that there was no one with that name in the family lineage. But I remained steadfast, and finally prevailed. The act seemed like a soothing antidote, for not long thereafter Cyprian, the late, stopped his vigil over my love-making.

As I look through the frill-curtained windows, there runs little Kapi, as I affectionately call my youngest son, chasing after his old car tyre, which he has christened Thunderbird.

RITUALS FOR MARTHA

Mmarita gave birth to her first child when she was seventeen. That did not cause a scandal in a township where sex was an addiction and childbearing nothing unusual among teenagers. If the newborns were girls, it soothed most families, because of the prospects of lobola. At least, that's what I thought until, after my marriage, I started attending funerals, burial society meetings and occasional weddings (for weddings were indeed a rarity in our township). I was a neighbour of Mmarita's parents.

It was always the younger participants who exhibited irritation at burial society meetings. Understandably so, when agenda items would be sacrificed so that the old people could indulge in their laments. Who could blame the young for becoming irritated? For it was they and their peers who were the chief subjects of these dirges. Fathers moaned about sons who were lazy, who seemed to enjoy no occupation except fathering kids. Mothers bemoaned their daughters whose heads were filled with boys and whose cleverness was only realised in dark alleys, where they let boys strain the tissues of their firm breasts until they were left sagging. Who could blame those old people for lamenting, when girls forgot to kindle fires at five o'clock, forgot to attend to their pots around six or seven, and wasted precious time and youth staring into the eyes of boys?

'What! Not only boys. Wena! Those girls are wanton. They are not ashamed of undressing men old enough to be their fathers.'

'It wasn't like that in our time, Mmawena.'

'Ohoo! Do you think there are any men left? These boys are not scared of leaving a child with a suckling baby.'

It was a perpetual cycle. Fathers blaming mothers and mothers blaming fathers, each accusing the other of either spoiling the children or not teaching them manners. Sometimes, those accusations and counter-accusations resulted in beatings. Some even developed into fist-fights as more and more women started asserting their independence. The fights at times made their way into our local newspaper. And we would relish those stories, making press cuttings which we would photocopy and circulate.

But at the same time, peace was quickly forged.

'How am I expected to cope? I am supporting not only my own children, but broods of these little bastards, whose mothers and fathers don't know the meaning of "support".'

'Let alone "work". How many of them have experienced the tyranny of waking up at four o'clock every weekday for a full nineteen-year stretch…?

'Don't you wonder why they settle for "vat en sit"? Useless bastards – can't afford lobola.'

'Hear this one: my son asked for money to buy bread the other day. You know what I said to him? "Buti! You are a man. If you can so quickly master child-making, boy, you are man enough to learn the art of money-making."'

'Yours is better, Rra Tommy. Mine is always borrowing money for taxi fares – to where? I don't know. So yesterday he came again: "Er… ou lady, ke vraiza tiger daa…" "What?" "I said, can you lend me ten rands?" he repeated. "Hau! You surprise me. Wasn't it you last week who was boasting about having bought a leather suit worth three thousand rands?" Hee! After that he tucked his tail between his legs and disappeared.'

Sometimes these conversations, or rather laments, would be punctuated with roars of laughter. From a distance, one would think the old people were enjoying the rewards of life.

As I have already said, Mmarita's childbearing did not cause a scandal. Though what it led to, some years later, would be a scandal of unparalleled proportions in the whole township. A dozen daring priests introduced it into their sermons. Burial society meetings digressed from their agendas to ponder it.

But why begin at the end?

Mmarita's real name was Martha, but everybody called her Mmarita, an Africanised version. Her aunt, Aunty Pheladi, who was known to have been schooled only up to standard three, was said to be the source of this name change. She was also known to be possessed by ancestral spirits. It was said that this would have led to her becoming a diviner or medium, if she hadn't failed her initiation rituals. She'd then been advised by her muti mentor to select somebody in the family, preferably a female, to replace her. And she chose Mmarita.

When Mmarita was a pretty little baby, her mother composed a lullaby for her:

Mmarita – yoo, Mmarita –
Kgarebe tsa geso di sa yo tansa
dikgekolo le dikgalabje di
boa ka madila…
Kgarebe tsa geso di sa you tansa
masogana le baditi
ba boa ka dikosa-thunsa-lerule
Mmarita – yoo, Mmarita –
Kgadi-ya-mma tsea lebese

That song is now forgotten. The voices that used to render it are tuneless. The ears that used to be enraptured by its soothing melodies are now deaf, sealed by the oily wax that has been accumulating since childhood. The song was forgotten even as Mmarita grew up, her ears readjusting to other frequencies: the rasping voices of males. The bearers of these voices came with different presentations – some sly and evasive, some soft and suggestive, others confident and persuasive, still others confused and hesitant. But their tune was the same.

Mmarita's curiosity was fuelled when she heard older women laughing: 'Hahaa! Ora Jacky. He couldn't even finish one sentence without biting his tongue…'

'Not my Ruben – that one! On our first night together, he kept rushing to the toilet with a running stomach. I took pity on the poor thing and pretended to fall asleep. And you know what, he came creeping to bed... and had a peaceful sleep. The running stomach miraculously cured.'

Mmarita took up with one boy of sixteen. She wondered how the 'poor thing' would make his proposition – and how he would behave on their first night together.

By then she was twelve. It was at this stage that Aunty Pheladi resolved to start preparing her niece for her future role. She needed to inform the girl what undergoing initiation as a medium, and getting approval of the ancestors, entailed. The first rule was chastity, until the trainee graduated. Thereafter, one had to observe a strict code of abstinence at certain times.

Of course, these were extremely complex issues for a girl who savoured soap operas, her favourites being *Loving* and *The Bold and the Beautiful*. No sexual contact the night before attending to a patient... Ridge and Brooke drowning in passion... no lustful thoughts when attending to male patients... Ava and Jack smouldering with desire... and she was to be a vessel for ancestral spirits!

But it seemed Aunty Pheladi never properly communicated her choice of Mmarita to the ancestors, for no ancestral communiqués were transmitted to Mmarita. She carried on with her life like any other young girl. She marvelled at seeing her breasts swell. When she was fourteen, she panicked at seeing blood flow out of her body, until her cousin introduced her to sanitary pads. Thus she graduated from being a township 'sqwaka', who uses folds of toilet paper, to being an 'ousie'. She then naturally stopped talking about boys with girls who still used folded toilet paper. She also started curling her hair and wearing jeans.

All these things troubled Aunty Pheladi.

'Aowa, don't worry. She's simply sampling life,' said one of Mmarita's neighbours.

'Mma-wena! Mothers always say that – "She's sampling life". Next time you see them – eyes rolling in their sockets, bellies swollen and tongues stiff against their palates.'

How sad and true it was. More and more young girls were swelling and bulging, the sad reality fermenting inside them. It was at such times that parents acknowledged that lobola was as elusive as a son-in-law. It was also then that they awakened to the fact that little Dorah or Phuti or Lerato was a failure. The girls, in turn, confirmed their failure as parents. And their parents would wait for the next burial society meeting, silently rehearsing their sad tales. There, they would bow their heads as they listened to each other pouring out sorrow and disappointment in their daughters, on whom they had placed all their hopes. Some would lament the price society was paying for its drive to progress. And all would wish they had only sons. At that point, parents whose sons were culprits would pretend their ears were itching and would start scratching them with matchsticks or grass stalks until that part of the conversation was over.

Mmarita started making evening excursions, supposedly to attend neighbourhood study groups. The glow that permeated her face on her return would tell another story, though.

'Mmarita ngwanaka, please my child, take care. You are the only one your father and I have. Not all the sweet melodies in the valleys originate from the lips of larks. Always remember that malnourished snakes also learn to sing so as to entice their prey. And some of them appear in the form of men.'

Of course, Mmarita repeated her mother's counsel to her friends. They burst into laughter. One or two repeated the words to their boyfriends.

Their boyfriends did not laugh, though. They just stroked their darlings affectionately, and repeated with emphasis the need for them to be open and confide in each other, as true lovers are supposed to do.

Throughout the neighbourhood, the girls' '*Hihihiii!*' would be heard. Then the boys' '*Kwa-kwaaakwaaaa!*' – almost sadistic laughter emanating from fragile vocal chords already starting to rust from cigarette and alcohol abuse.

The young people in our township did not regard making love while standing a disgrace. But the older people viewed it with contempt. 'What kind of offspring will come out of such copulation?' they sneered. They insisted that young people should wait until after marriage.

But waiting was anathema to young people. It was as if they suspected that death would rob them of the pleasures that love had in store. The forbidden honeycomb was too tempting to resist, and daring each other to taste it became a second hobby, after truancy.

Mmarita got tired of her teenage boyfriend. She gave the reason that she was tired of 'hitch-hiking', for that is what young people in our township called vertical lovemaking. She also confided in her friends that she was bored with her young lover: 'A ke sa di kena, he is always nervous and hurried, looking over his shoulder and ready to run whenever he hears or sees someone approaching.'

How could he not be? He was not sure when Mmarita's mother or father might apprehend them. Or when one of the older 'toughies' might bump into them, pump a bullet through his head and 'jackroll' his Mmarita.

In his place, she got herself a taxi-driver. Luckily he owned a backyard shack, which proved cosy for their intimate sessions. Like all girls of her generation, and those before, and probably even those to come, she knew it was hard to come by a millionaire in the townships; but divine intervention could still deliver her own personal chauffeur. Besides, Mmarita had to get herself a taxi-driver boyfriend because all her friends had one. For them it meant graduation into a higher social order. Of course, they looked down upon those who still dated schoolboys, even if they used sanitary pads and curled their hair as well.

What was the bait? A miniskirt? Tight-fitting pants? A pretty face? Wrong! Every girl growing up knew the mentality of taxi-drivers. What worked was to play-act coyness and delicacy, and frequent their haunts. Mmarita followed this advice to the letter. And so she got her 'Lunch Boy'.

True to his nickname, her taxi-driver would appear punctually every school-day around lunch time, bearing a package of Chicken Licken or Kentucky. Later on, she informed him that the now thing was Nando's. That added an extra four kilometres of detour from his main route. But, like any solicitous lover, he endured. His Sundays were given over to transporting her and her friends to Moretela Park. He knew it was a detour the taxi owner wouldn't approve of, but the yearning lover in him gave him a sense of adventure and boldness.

And the old people continued with their laments:

'This Moretela Park of theirs! Kare, it is their new-found church.'

'I say, they can't even afford lobola, but are wasteful on these Moretela Park outings of theirs.'

Who could blame the old people? Theirs was an era long effaced from the brow of reality, an illusion they occasionally brought back to life in memory, a rainbow diluted by the tears of lamenting gods.

What a shame! The girl who was at the forefront of a generation of fornicators was tired of vertical love-making. She should not have scorned it, though, for that was exactly the position she was in three years later when she conceived. The physical features of her baby confirmed speculation that children conceived vertically suffered defects. Just to be sure, dozens of people thronged to her place to see the baby.

Afterwards, some of them started spreading the rumour that at birth the infant had been as upright as a reed. Some even said his little penis maintained an erection, which collapsed soon after someone mentioned the little bastard's father by name. Agaa! Who can believe those township gossip-mongers?

The first reaction of Aunty Pheladi on hearing that Mmarita was pregnant was to consider rushing her for an abortion. But then she recalled that nothing can be hidden from the ancestors. And she knew that her pretty niece was lost: 'Like Jezebel! Like Lot's wife! She will suffer the vengeance of the gods.'

And there was nothing mortal man could do to save her. All diviners shied away from her, for they declared tampering with her would be akin to challenging the ancestors. Like Prometheus, her heart would feed the wild birds of prey.

Like Joan of Arc, her flesh and bones would kindle the greatest bonfire.

I used to be one of the many sceptics about such prophecies of doom. We were justified in this: hadn't we grown up on the precipice of an apocalypse, orated to by Watchtower evangelists throughout the years? Warnings that had not only been proved wrong, but had also turned the messengers into buskers and their testimony into a mockery. I held firmly to my doubts until 1982. That is when I saw a man being roasted with three tyres around him. Later, I saw mongrels fighting over parts of his charred remains. Then, in those dark days, it dawned on me that my perceptions might be only as solid as the rainbow. The world might well be coming to a fiery end.

Like all reluctant grandparents, Mmarita's parents had a grudging fondness for their grandchild. Fate decided that they would become his legal guardians, for a couple of weeks after the birth, Mmarita was knocked over by a car on her way from Kwa Muhle, where she had gone to file a paternity suit. Her taxi-driver disappeared, and resurfaced months later, driving around with one of her friends.

Initially we thought she had been committed to an institution. But no – it was only that she was never seen venturing out except at night. It was Aunt Pheladi who ended up at Witkoppen. It started with her exclaiming over the tragic fate of her niece. When two hours had elapsed and she was still mumbling the same words, a sangoma was called. After a couple of minutes with the patient, she told the family that there was nothing she could do.

A long consultation followed. Some of the relatives recommended taking her to Giyani, others said Mozambican muti-men were better equipped to handle such a case. It was at the mention of taking her to Phafula, great muti-man of the Northern Transvaal, that Aunt Pheladi stood up and bolted. Two days later, the traffic police apprehended her marching up and down the Ben Schoeman Highway. She was naked, still lamenting the fate of her niece.

The first sighting of Mmarita, or rather her silhouette, occurred at twenty to nine on the night of the twelfth of April, 1987. It was on the eighth anniversary of her self-exile into darkness.

Her son, Kgetsi, was then of course eight years old. It was as though she had never existed for him. When asked about her, he would always respond by talking about his grandmother.

'No – I mean your mother, your real mother.'

He would pause, thinking through the question again. 'Mmmm… my mother, she is at work. She does washing and ironing piece-jobs.'

Kgetsi didn't suffer a complex though, as most people feared. He was an adventurous, daring boy. Maybe that was the cause of his downfall.

Together with other boys his age, he would taunt and jeer at young girls. That was understandable. They were past the age of playing husbands and wives, fathers and mothers. And they asserted their 'bigness' with the girls. During playtime they were now preoccupied with TV heroes like Zorro and MacGyver. However, they always got confused when these heroes of theirs expressed attraction to pretty women. This dilemma was solved by the bright Kgetsi. He called a council and reviewed the play rules. He employed his eloquence to win over the other boys, despite their doubts. Soon his proposal was accepted by all.

'Yaa! There is Mantwa. There is Zodwa. There is Thembi. From today, they will be our women.'

And he chose for himself the fairest, Zodwa. She was nine then.

On the sly, he got the girls to accompany the boys to a run-down, abandoned house. There they had the time of their childhood. Playing familiar and recently invented games... until the beckoning of the serious game, the one that men and women play in their bedrooms.

It was probably curiosity that led Zodwa to take off her panties. It was probably the same curiosity that led Kgetsi to take off his underpants.

'Let us do it like they always do on TV.'

They were still marvelling at the strange and funny sensation of each other's bodies when Mmarita pounced on them. She went for Kgetsi's throat and started squeezing. It was the first time in eight years that she had ventured out in broad daylight, while her parents were at work. Trailing behind her were some of the neighbours.

When they managed to free the little boy from her grip he was already unconscious and frothing. Later, the neighbours saw his limp body being hoisted onto a stretcher by frantic ambulance attendants. Still later, they told the police they had first been alerted by Mmarita's screaming: 'Get off me... *get off meee!!!*'

LAST PARADE AT GOLGOTHA

Ondangwa realised he was extremely exhausted, although he was not yet at his destination. That was strange, considering it was a mere three kilometres; in the past he had easily made that sort of distance. At times he had doubled, even trebled, that. Why this odd feeling today? He shrugged at the thought that it might be old age.

Thirty-five was, indeed, old age – it was a miraculous achievement for a young man to reach such an age these days. Yes, mankind was about to follow the dinosaurs into extinction. Maybe the world would soon be populated and ruled by ants and little bacteria, which sustain themselves on almost nothing.

With the many forces lurking to snatch away one's life, it was apparent that the odyssey of living was ended before it began. If these forces were not human-inspired, like witchcraft, car accidents or murder, then they were natural disasters like droughts, starvation, floods or earthquakes.

Ondangwa could not decide how to classify AIDS, but concluded the disease was certainly a curse on human survival and progression. And possibly the ultimate curse on the sex act itself. It was a fulfilment of the biblical prophecy of Apocalypse. End of the world through fire... fire of loins.

Before going deeper into these thoughts, Ondangwa felt the skin of his soles start to burn. On closer scrutiny, he noticed corns and blisters. Why, he could not understand, for he washed and scrubbed his feet every day. In fact, his morning bath was said to last a full sixty minutes. This had always been source of conflict between himself and his mother-in-law. She eventually managed to influence his wife. Days later, he noticed that Ntsiki was starting to fill his bath with less and less water. Moreover, the water was becoming cooler and cooler. But this did not affect his bath duration; instead it widened the rift between them.

Ag shame! Of all worldly treasures, the woman chose to horde water. Stingy woman! What uniqueness was there in water, after all? An element with which you couldn't even rinse your sins. Although there was the baptismal ritual, which was supposed to erase one's previous sins and make one new-born. Some said 'Born Again'. Then he remembered the communion. He wondered at times if the sacrament wasn't just an excuse to indulge in drink. What was this fascination with liquid among Christians? Could it be that their faith was not strong enough to be tested on a bed of red-hot coals, like the Hindus'? He recalled the case of the Samaritan harlot who denied Jesus water. For stinginess, she had earned a curse from the Son of Man. Maybe Ntsiki was some remote cousin or even latter-day reincarnation of that Samaritan harlot. He wished he could curse her...

As a Catholic, he did not believe in divorce. Or care much to divorce over a mere bath. But that was exactly what his mother advised him to do.

'Beat her at least,' she advised again.

'But Mme! That's taking it too far...'

'Taking it too fa-aar, wwhaaat?' she responded, fuming. 'Wasn't that five thousand they demanded for lobola too much?... Yerreee! Ngwana-ke-wena-wa-reng!'

Ondangwa looked deep in his mother's eyes. He saw his own reflection and started thinking about his childhood, the days of his youth. Both relatives and complete strangers used to say how much he looked like her, and that he shared her character traits. But he knew he wasn't like her. When he looked in her eyes, he tried to see himself – or the specks that were supposed to represent her in him, or him in her. But there were none. The only thing he did manage to see was his own reflection, a tiny blob shrunk to the size of a pin by her iris… his esteemed masculinity and ego dwarfed, rendered insignificant by her fragile feminine iris.

Even at thirty-five, he realised, he remained an infant in her eyes, an infant she would mother until the grave relieved her of that burden. And that made him feel extremely vulnerable. He had tried to overcome that by falling in love with her eyes. Not only hers, but also those of other women. And eyes had ended up constituting the epitome of feminine sensuality and erotic passion for him. Throughout his life, they would wield hypnotic power over him.

The spell would only be broken ten years later, when he was hanged with a burning tyre around his neck, having been sentenced to death by a 'People's Court' in Alexandra. (Maybe the act would have been gratifying had it occurred in reality – pity that it was only enacted in the recesses of his mind, where his conscience was struggling to come to terms with the realities of the times.) Up to the last moment, his eyes were glued to those of a twenty-one-year-old virgin, one of the weeping spectators. Crying! An emotional act that is slowly wringing the world dry. It is only organisms that are incapable of this act that are destined to inherit the earth. Despite his proclaimed supremacy, man's ability to shed tears cancels his status as lord over other living creatures – a status that has eluded him since creation. Hasn't man, armed with knowledge, matured enough to recognise crying for what it is – a trifle, a nonsensical expression of happiness or tragedy that is draining the world of the moistness and dampness it so desperately needs?

He recalled how his father regularly used to beat his mother. Never understanding or appreciating her big, moist eyes, he would beat her terribly, so that she usually ended up with 'blue eyes'. That would happen, in particular, after his father had drunk four or six pints at Auntie Kikilha's.

His mother was different from other women in the township. During those terrible beatings, she never cried or attracted attention. She never screamed or ran outside, but would obediently submit herself, bent or kneeling before her husband, pleading or mumbling his praise-poems and totem.

He recalled how he'd once tried to intervene by snatching the broomstick from his father.

'Hey-wena ngwana tena! Bring that back!' his mother had yelled at him.

'I won't, I won't… he's killing you,' he'd tried to reason with her.

But it was to no avail. She would hobble after him, take the broomstick and give it back to her husband, who would resume his punishment.

Nx! Why was he thinking about all that? He couldn't find a reason, except that he was putting his mind through the dark alleys of his childhood; alleys with sore and sticky edges. He only knew that he was extremely exhausted.

It was that damning state of exhaustion that had driven him to trains and taxis. But he'd started missing his long walks, missing the pedestrian's unbridled monopoly of the roads and arrogance towards motorists. Train rides irritated him. Crowding, pick-pocketing and shoe trampling were the rule.

Reluctantly, his mind drifted to one memorable ride, years ago…

'Exhausted, like a donkey… no, like a mongrel. No, like a farmhand… or maybe like a tokoloshe,' he mumbled softly.

'Are you talking?' the young woman sitting next to him on the train asked.

'What... err... why?' he stammered.

'I heard something about tokoloshe,' she continued.

Clearly, she was in the mood for talking.

'Damn,' he muttered. He was not in that mood. He also noticed she'd stopped pretending to read a copy of *True Love* magazine. It occurred to him that she was in the mood for being proposed to... 'Damn!' He was not in that mood either.

He realised his ankles were strained. He become conscious of the fact that even his knees were creaking. 'Agg! Why doesn't this bloody train have an accident...'

An outcry erupted from his fellow commuters. 'Whaaaat!!' one voice echoed.

'Whyyy?!' two others chorused.

'Accident! Afa ga o moloi wena,' another accused.

The whole compartment was staring at him in shock. Why? He hadn't messed his trousers. No, neither had he urinated in his trousers, nor was his fly open. Why... no, neither was his 'small boy' excitedly outstretched alongside his thighs. He noticed that even the Watchtower mobile evangelist was in shocked silence, the koppie-dice game abandoned halfway.

'Damn it! I didn't say that aloud,' he told himself. But he should have known. His mind and senses were so numb they were reacting mechanically, rambling on by themselves. Mental lethargy was upon him, mercilessly collaring and dragging him to the scrapyard.

He began thinking about Ntsiki. Her shabby appearance. Her flabby shape. Her grouchy company. Her ever-increasing disregard for basic hygiene... and the young woman who was sitting next to him. The young woman who was in the mood for being talked to... the young woman who was conscious and proud of her appearance, who also was in the mood for being proposed to... the young woman whose eyes were like almonds, like a radiant sunflower. Regretful thoughts about his five-thousand-rand lobola weren't that far behind.

'Yerreee! Pshooo!!' He puffed deeply. Yaa! Maybe Bra Ntikzo was right: 'Leave the magogo home, ntwana maan! Check bana outie maan! Nothing better than bana en s'putla.' Yaa! That was Ntikzo talk.

Nx! Bugger-off, Bra Ntikzo and his twak. Why should he care, Ondangwa reasoned. Sapped of energy as he was, human existence was reduced to a mere fraction of a feeling – a feeling of exhaustion. He became aware that his mind was operating at low gear. In laborious chugs and pauses. And his vision was becoming more and more blurred. Mirages and stars appeared with unabashed exhibitionism.

He fumbled for his cigarettes. Eshoooo! He'd got none. How about trying some fellow puffer...
'Skeif daar, broer?'

'Eeii! Broer, ke draai.'

Agaa! He was tired of having to grovel, to lick others' shoes for 'nkauza'.

'O-yaa!' The smokers' brotherhood and solidarity was fast dying. One hardly got even a stompie...

'Nx! Bongame fela!' He shot up and moved to another coach. 'What's wrong with you fucking, bloody, filthy train commuters!'

His eyes fell on the red-sprayed graffiti on the coach walls. Then he noticed that underneath was pencilled:

'Yu were fuking! bloody! having yur senses sarender to your erekshin when you rote thes – thes is no fuking puplic toilet.'

It occurred to Ondangwa that he would have to visit all the public toilets in Johannesburg to view all the graffiti. Maybe that way he might come across some creativity. Rebellious creativity from society's oppressed individuals. Those like him, but who didn't utter their wayward statements, but preferred to paint, scribble or spray them on public walls.

Then his eyes fell on a young man, a bearded animal. They were animals, that he was certain of, despite protestations the other might have offered. Animals destined for extinction, culled by their own civilisation. He noticed the Peter Stuyvesant dangling from the other's lips. He grinned, exposing his own nicotine-stained teeth. But the other turned aside.

He started biting his lips. Then he licked them and swallowed a trickle of blood… Ntsiki, portly as ever. She was probably busy with her unappetising pots on the coal stove…

Tshoooo! He yawned and stretched himself. No, it wasn't his body that was exhausted. It was a feeling that emanated from deep within his heart.

If human existence was fatigue of both the mind and body, Silenus was probably right when he advised King Midas that the most desirable thing for mankind was not to be born at all, or alternatively to die soon. Still walking, Ondangwa felt the urge to continue living dissipate. There was no regret or remorse though – he realised that in all his walks, extremely exhausting walks, he'd been going nowhere. Remote, beyond his immediate and possible reach, was life and love decked on a giant table, with a great blue tablecloth and giant golden serviettes. Only with telescopic sight could he peep with malnourished longing at that splayed scenery. But would he reach it? Didn't Moses falter at Mount Pisgah? Gibran also sought eternal rest in New York. And Icarus at Crete. Then there was Modjadji, the first rainmaker, she too finally sought the company of the ancestors at Ga-Modjadji. Darwin, who embraced mortality at Down. No, not even Bedford Forrest could bear the Klan Cross beyond, but had to surrender it at Pulaski. Not even the mystic poet himself, Saint John of the Cross, could sustain himself; he too had to seek eternal solitude with his God at Ubeda.

And with shocked finality, he realised that in all his long walks, the meadow he'd thought he was journeying towards was in fact a valley of death, the final resting place, layered with multiple mirrors for self-reflection, self-appreciation and self-indulgence. Biding its time, waiting to crush its tenants. To smash them to smithereens.

Then the awakening took possession of him. He matured instantly as knowledge enfolded him. Then he aged. He could see he was the odd, and at times even bothersome cockroach, ant, bedbug or mosquito that arrogantly prances around, trespassing on prohibited sacred grounds.

STREET FEATURES

THE STREET COULD BE ANYWHERE. It stretches along an even gradient, punctuated by four-way junctions every five hundred metres or so. At longer intervals there are robots that maintain guard night and day. But, like any other mechanical thing, they become sick once in a while, so that instead of their electric winks and blinkings, the traffic is confronted by their human counterparts. But these too, like anything mortal, are prone to error – with the result that stretches of crawling motorcars idle and doze in that outstretched path. For in fact it is a path, like any in the bush, except that this one is decorated with tar, granite paving, and permanent yellow and white markings…

This is the street I dreamed about and longed for throughout my childhood. But now we are estranged. It has become possessed by four-wheeled chameleons, snails, sparrows, eagles, sharks and whales, some of them belching loudly and puffing smog from their narrow nostrils. Kites I longed to manoeuvre and chase after in its wide skies have been displaced, mocked by helicopters, gliders, aeroplanes and all sorts of mechanical monsters that overwhelm and dwarf everything else up there.

This is a street I don't dream of anymore. It is now sandwiched between tall buildings, most of them not less than seven storeys high. Often it slides a little way into squalor, but then municipality sanitation officers remember it. Kind-heartedly, they retrieve it from complete disintegration. This is usually on Saturday evenings or Sunday afternoons. Of course, it does get a nightly scrubbing, in the shape of garbage removal every evening around eight. Still, like a self-indulgent pig, it is back to its former state the following day, immediately after lunch time. I conclude that spring-cleaning for this street is hopeless.

My first observation, on seeing the street again after nearly ten years, was that it could be anywhere. It could be heaven, travelled by the few who've attained salvation. Or even hell, strewn with the multitudes of those who've flouted salvation – the revelry-drugged mob, swarming like ants around jam or bees over honey.

This view isn't mine alone, for those who see, use and abuse the street every day, over and over again, are of the same verdict.

'But the path to heaven is narrow... doesn't the bible testify to that?'

'Ya! That was before the clever ones died. The ones with an IQ of 150. They have probably introduced grinders and caterpillars there as well.'

'That's sickening blasphemy.'

'Don't you agree, heaven too needs to be modernised? Otherwise it would lose potential recruits to places like Sun City. Boy, flesh merchants have also awoken to the dangers of AIDS. They prescribe condoms. And that's modernisation. I don't see any reason why heaven shouldn't go for a face-lift as well.'

'Alley to social utopia!' bold newspaper headlines might shout.

'Red-light main road to moral degradation!' moralists might pronounce with condemnation.

Certainly the street is confused — just like all those who walk or drag themselves over its granite and tar. Going westward, one always has the unsettling feeling of approaching a lion's den, maybe because of the hot, smelly air that drifts from that direction. It is also like ascending an extremely steep hill. But going eastward is like fleeing a horde of living corpses with iron clamps chained to your ankles. It is a gentle down-slope, but the drag!

Some say it is a bewitched street. Others attribute its strangeness to perennial tremors caused by geological forces in its bowels. Still others say there is a natural pool underneath the street, where a great serpent lives. Its breathing is the cause of all the abnormal feelings people experience there.

The street also witnesses the birth of boys and girls. In adolescence they discover each other, drawn by the magnetic force that emanates from their loins. They become acquainted, become husbands and wives, and start copulating. Little children, some resembling them and others not resembling them, are born. Then age starts mistreating the children as they grow to adulthood. It is then that some choose to return to the rural areas, while others are hastily claimed by the grave.

It was here that the longing to meet a girl first took root in me. But because of my erratic stay, I was unable to stretch my roots deep enough for them to entangle and intertwine with those of a girl.

Were you to stop and inspect the street more appreciatively, you would see it differently. It is the kind of street that goes straight to wooing, grabbing and clinging onto your affections. At one angle, it appears shaped like a maiden's torso. And men of all ages are in one way or another infatuated with that. There are times it appears like a Michelangelo sculpture, and women are ever consumed with trying to remodel their husbands' and boyfriends' age-battered and life-battered bodies on it.

At times I have seen young men, probably lonely ones, lie prostrate on its alabaster slabs. They weep silently, or roll around. Sometimes they behave obscenely, rocking themselves up and down. Embarrassed passers-by realise they are simulating love-making.

'Disgusting! Why don't they go buy it in Hillbrow.'

Young women strolling with their boyfriends turn against them when walking on that street. Trouble starts when they first insist on taking off their shoes.

'He-wena! Ke eng tse, hee?'

'Let's lie down.'

'Lie down! Where? Why?'

'Isn't it romantic? To let the wind caress you. To feel the pavement whisper and tickle your feet.'

The boyfriends then either drag their girls away or slap them. But one or two try playing the game. And they pay the price. For, once down, the girls' attention is diverted — scribbling on the concrete what the boyfriends call nonsense, like 'Sex me up' or 'Shake-shake-shake, shake your body,' and similar song lyrics. After that they kiss the slab, whispering how gentle its touch is on their bodies, cooing how sweet it is. And the inference is quickly picked up by the boyfriends, even the dull ones:

'You mean I don't satisfy you, ne?'

Or: 'Look here, Kedi! I don't dig your attitude.'

'Huwii! Listen, he doesn't dig my attitude. What attitude is that, dear?'

'Kedi! Don't get funny, ne!' Whaaaa! – and a klap puts a stop to the women's funniness.

No! The street was never a piece of architectural genius. On closer inspection, especially with a microscope or magnifying glass, one notices little cracks here and there. There are bigger crevices in unsuspected places. These are places of refuge or asylum, where cents from the poor and rich alike are likely to wedge, therein to embrace posterity. They are spared the abuse of sweaty palms.

No! The street was never a piece of inspired technological engineering either. In many places, its edges have given in to the pressures of shoes and car tyres. Careless drunkards now and then sprain ankles or even break fingers. A dozen naughty kids are always available to testify to the foul mood and erratic behaviour of that street. Their bruised knees and foreheads and missing teeth are witness to that.

But the street has its patrons, lots and lots of them. The plain, the odd, the attractive, the rowdy and ugly ones.

In the old days, Saturday afternoons meant 'woza weekend'. The inhabitants would creep out from their holes: labourers' top-floor rooms, ground-floor store-rooms... and on Sunday evenings they would disappear, to hole up again until the next weekend. At that point, when they chose to dematerialise, you would be unlikely to trace them. Even with the assistance of giant searchlights. For they had learned to evade the clutches of the Group Areas Act. It was at night that one could hear them whispering in muffled tones as they stole to deserted elevators, or indulged themselves in the pleasures of forbidden love.

Their life began after five, when the office workers and their bosses were gone. Then they would emerge, mothers with legions of children hanging on their aprons. Children whose fathers had forgotten their existence. Husbands with long-forgotten, rural wives; sons and daughters with bundu-confined parents. Again they would materialise. Appendages, human relics relegated to social scrap-heaps. With the setting of the sun they would emerge: gangs of women reduced to selling their bodies for survival; vulture-like young men haunting bags, purses and pockets; vagrants terrorising dustbins and rubble piles for edibles.

After ten years, I came back, hoping to rekindle my acquaintance with the street. To end our estrangement and take up where we left off. Instead I met her...

Her name was Palesa, she told me. Her age was twenty-three. Her place of birth was Tsomo. In the Transkei, she added. I asked about her occupation. She looked me deep in the eyes, but would not tell. Her stare was bold, challenging, yet femininely sensuous. In the mirror-like centre of her eyes, I saw childhood dreams gone wrong. Ambitions misdirected by ignorance and hopes betrayed by realities. I saw a whole existence derailed, immature ears crowded by a barrage of manipulative words – the snakes and ladders game of adolescence.

After a while she relaxed. She told me of the male cousins she stayed with. Then I noticed her bosom. It was limp, like a deflated balloon.

It bore witness to an untimely motherhood. A motherhood that overnight had shuttled her from the harmonies of girlhood to the battering perils of single parenthood; that had served as a passport to exile. Away from the verbal abuse of parents, the scorn of neighbours and peers. From the jeers and sneers of former boyfriends. She had sought and found comfort in flight; whereupon the unknown had taken pity on her, welcomed and consoled her.

It was then that I realised everything she had told me about herself was not true – yet she was not a liar. She was a weaver of words. Words woven around her fragile inner being. Like Scheherazade, cheating loneliness and death by inventing stories of hope. Narrating them to herself. Constantly weaving courage, daring the possibilities of AIDS and other sexually transmitted diseases.

Two weeks later, I went to the corner on which we'd met. She was not there. I asked around for her. None of the girls seemed to know her. Her name was unfamiliar to most. I gave a short but desperate description, and then a few recalled her. I noted that in some of those recollections were evident both pleasure and spite, while in others I noticed pity.

'I last saw her with a white man in a red Sierra,' one of the girls told me.

'No-no! It was a black man in a grey Golf,' another insisted.

Did it matter or make any difference? Palesa, Melisa, or whoever she was, was nowhere. I noticed that some of the girls were eyeing me suspiciously, while others exhibited salespersons' interest, as if I might be persuaded into a deal. Finally, overcome by both uneasiness and pity, I turned away from them. Slowly I dragged myself westwards. My eyes would now and then fasten on distant female figures and fish around their profiles for familiar features. At times my gaze would hook onto kerb-crawling cars. Would she emerge from that car? Was it her, that one tucking her legs into the front seat?

My ears sucked onto familiar sounds: distant laughter, whistles, motorcar hooters. Would she emerge in a dazed rush for that one particular, favourite client? Would that car hooter or whistle nurse her from her sick-bed or intensive care unit… or awaken her from the grave?

Where are you, dear one?

Would she tear free from the clutches of a new client for the customary caresses of her consistent client? Yet I knew I did not have the power or resources to rescue her. I couldn't re-dress the stage to offer her a better act. An act devoid of those beds, the posturing, the life-consuming embraces. Palesa or Melisa, or whoever she was, was no longer there. No more a feature of the street.

I fumbled along that merciless street. Now and then my vision would blur, and it was in such a state that she would become clearer... the one woman I might have loved. The one woman whose roots might have intertwined with mine to form a nourishing tree for little boys and girls of our own. That would have been possible, in another time and other circumstances.

In the end, she merged with the other insignificant particles of that street – artlessly laid granite paving-stones, hurriedly levelled tar. Fresh and rain-stained cigarette stubs. Tastelessly graffitied walls and corners permeated with sulphuric urine odour. And here and there, orange and banana peels strewn around.

DEATH AND THE PALMIST

(*Letter from the dead*)

IT WAS ON THE THIRD DAY OF THE incident that we braced ourselves for something sinister. Not that an itching palm was a riddle, something to shame the beards of our wisdom. We knew, though, that it was an omen. 'Incident' might not even be the appropriate term, but then, having chased the same sun behind the same trees and mountain for the better part of our lives, we were prone to employing hyperbole in our descriptions of everything, merely to give a semblance of significance to our monotonous lives.

And it was bound to happen that we individually and collectively bore grudges against Pontsho. Who was she, anyway, to pour scorn onto our communal pride? Pontsho ridiculed everything – our employment of riddles, hyperbole and jokes, our indulging in sorghum and marula beer, our morabaraba games and our habitual lounging in the shade after midday meals. All the while, we kept reminding her that these were mere diversions to lessen the burden of drudgery in our lives. She countered by accusing us of ineptitude and laziness, using a lot of other similarly degrading terms.

You will understand our triumph at what we later collectively referred to as 'Pontsho's affliction'. Pontsho, grouchy over a palm-itch, continuously scratching and scratching, like strumming a minute guitar. Or 'like a mongrel or pig with lekker krap,' someone intoned. For this comic relief, the speaker earned himself a gourd of frothing sorghum beer.

Our triumph was not gratifying, though, because Pontsho treated our making an issue out of her palm-itch with scorn: 'Come off it, you illiterates. None of you invented a fart or a belch. So stop pretending that you know my itching palm is a countdown to the end of the world.'

Our degree of shock prompted us to consult ngaka-ya-ditaola, for we all agreed only one bewitched could degenerate that badly in neighbourliness.

Pontsho's palm was not the only village issue. She was beautiful as well. The kind of bewitching beauty only angels or she-devils possess. What else could we term it? At a time when women's worth was the number of babies their wombs could produce or menial tasks their arms could carry out, she chose to parade the pains beauty was capable of inflicting.

All mothers in our village used to advise their marriageable sons: 'Mosadi ke tshwene, o lewa mabogo.' Prospective mothers-in-law pointed out that Pontsho's kind of beauty fed only the eyes while sucking out men's guts, rendering them zombies. We thought the mothers' warnings were motivated by female jealousy, until we started hearing rumours about bizarre behaviour by some of our brothers: boys, married men and old men were so besotted with Pontsho that they would wander about in the streets or nearby woods at full moon, crooning, chanting or whispering her name. Younger women were known to fall into stuttering and swooning spells in her presence. These afflictions were known to disappear when she withdrew.

It was because of this that some of us started believing certain preachers – that Pontsho was a she-devil incarnate, bent on corrupting Christian youths tantalised by her beauty, convinced she was the Madonna. Kgwedi, the village boomelaar, nearly started an inter-religious bloodbath between Catholics and Protestants by insisting that waters of everlasting life flowed between her legs – the idiot! The Protestant deserter forgot in his drunken stupor that the guzzler on his left was the local Catholic priest.

From those before us, we had learnt that when your palm itches, it is an omen. It means you will receive money – if you were owed, or perhaps if a rich uncle on his death-bed forgot you were worse than a piece of dog shit and decided to bequeath his entire estate to you. Or it means that a long-lost acquaintance will soon reappear, and you will shake his hand repeatedly. Relief will embrace you with the realisation that the cure for your itching palm has arrived.

We learnt of all the body's different signs and their interpretations. Itching foot-soles foretold travel, or being soaked in rain; a palpitating upper eyelid meant seeing a long-lost acquaintance; an itching lower eyelid foretold crying or mourning for a loved one. Then there was the best of all, choking on saliva – that foretold a feast. Most of us enjoyed this last sign. How could we not, when meat and other delicacies were scarce? It was only the occasional funeral that guaranteed us those treats.

Collective panic would set in if none of us reported such an omen. Then we would set about lamenting terrible times, a soup-drought for our palates.

As tradition demanded, we passed these signs on to our grandchildren as a legacy. Especially as there was little else we could show to them as proof of our having suckled from Mother Nature. It wasn't as if our grandchildren appreciated our wisdom. Word carried by bats and owls reached us about their condemnation of us as a generation of failures. We knew, and were powerless to reverse that... had we but left them herds of goats and cows, or mielie-fields, our failures would be erased.

With time, we became convinced that Pontsho was the prophetess of the generation of ridiculers, because all the young ones were starting to adopt her attitude.

Over frothing sorghum beer, we worked out counter-strategies. We ridiculed the young by pointing out that they conducted themselves that way because they were conceived during the day – yea! It was only dogs and donkeys that mated during daytime. Not surprising, then, that the offspring of drunkards and daytime fornicators behaved like animals.

After these strategising sessions, we would turn to our favourite songs:

> *Couzy-motswala is for sale*
> *Buy her and fill our bellies*
> *Tswang-tswang motswala*
> *Couzy-motswala is for sale*
> *Bed my wife, I'll bed yours...*

A new refrain was added to the popular ditty:

> *Tswang-tswang motswala*
> *motswala-ka ngwana malome*
> *kare ntsee oa gana*
> *Kgomo di boela sakeng...*
>
> *Come forth cousin*
> *cousin, beloved child of my uncle's*
> *marry me so cattle can remain in the*
> *family kraal*
> *but he refuses...*

Our days were spent in such humorous sentiment – until Pontsho started referring to 'poor old women and men's tales'.

'Did you hear that little witch? She refers to our warning regarding her palm-itch as –'

'Stop right there before curses follow you, to the seventh generation!' – so anybody daring to echo her blasphemy would be cautioned.

We all pointed out to her what would befall her, but Pontsho, being Pontsho, chose to dare our collective indignation, if not that of the ancestors. From that day onwards, we all waited with baited breath to witness Pontsho reaping the bitter rewards of disrespect for our customs.

Our anticipation was at fever point when we heard rumour that her palm-itch was getting itchier by the day.

We reasoned with her that to break the omen of death, maybe hers or that of someone close to her, she needed to act quickly. When it appeared that she was going to do nothing, we resolved to act. Our first action was to send children, little ones whom we reckoned hadn't yet committed sin. Their task was to scratch her palm, because that was the remedy we all applied when our palms itched. When that failed, we reasoned: 'You call those children – they are miniature monsters! No manners or shame in them. With the bad influence of those moving pictures they see, kare ruri you get little playground serial killers. At three they are already experts at torturing frogs, ants and dung-beetles. They also poke sticks, stones and all sorts of funny things in the rear ends of domestic animals.'

'Ka mma ruri, with chickens born with four legs. The world is truly nearing its end.'

At a village kgotla, we resolved a virgin was our next-best bet. Though we were all equally jealous of Pontsho, we were wholeheartedly united in our effort to shield her from a destructive fate. Although we were preoccupied with seeing her humiliated and humbled, secretly we knew that we did not want her to die from the curse.

After patiently waiting for one parent, just one, to volunteer his or her child, panic broke out when that seemed unlikely to happen. We were all shocked to realise that moral decadence in the village was so bad that not a single virgin boy or girl could be found among hundreds of children and teenagers. Some jumped in to cite this as the reason the village was experiencing so much drought of late.

We probably would have sat there the whole day if Mme-Makgatho had not come dragging her mentally retarded eighteen-year-old daughter. Relief loosened our tongues. The customary riddles, jokes and anecdotes followed. In our excitement, we formed a guard of honour to lead the dribbling girl to Pontsho's compound.

'Why abuse the poor thing?' Pontsho jeered.

'Homola wena, be grateful that we share in your suffering.'

'What! Call an itching palm an affliction? You backward natives.'

Maybe, in fairness, we might indeed be termed backward natives, but being called that by a woman – well, a girl really, and an unmarried one for that matter – was extreme; a trampling, trivialisation and spitting-on of the manhoods hanging between our legs. A couple of grouchy men were about to let their tempers descend to the level of their ridiculed manhoods, but we pointed out to them that, as always, arguing with Pontsho was like pissing in your sorghum beer – an act that not only spoils the beer, but your day as well. We all agreed that such time would be more productively utilised guzzling down our beloved wives' brews.

Some of us enjoyed provoking her like this, especially during ploughing season, when the sun conspired with our lazy limbs to usher in yet another harvest shortfall. We nonetheless got Mapule to scratch Pontsho's palm. That night, none of us slept as we raced the night to a new day. While we kept vigil outside her house, Pontsho had a good night's sleep.

Despite the warnings by a village elder that the sun would rise draped in an unusually red halo, the third day of our suspense dawned like any other. The cocks crowed at the usual time, the dawn breeze sprayed the roofs of our huts with dew, calves demanded their succour at the right times. And we were reminded of Nongqawuse and her dream-interpreting uncle, Mhlagaza. But our dreams were different. We dreamt that the mielie-fields tended themselves, that benevolent spirits did the reaping, grinding and cooking for us, that our enemies turned into cow dung so that we could fertilise our fields. Those dreams were fed by our longing to spend more time duelling with ants, beetles and flies for the shade.

Our disappointment in seeing the sun rise without any unusual red halo led us dejectedly to our different compounds. We started counselling each other: 'Patience, patience, bathong. The day is still young. Who knows, irresponsible midwives might still sour our celebrations with news of a stillborn.' That was the kind of language we all wanted to hear: it gave comfort, it promised drama.

Our dread of ongoing boredom was broken at midday, when news reached us that Pontsho's palm was itching again. Like bees heeding the call of their queen, we converged on her compound. For wasn't that what she had become, a queen? An umbilical cord threaded its way from her navel through her palm to the core of our brains.

Once again, we were united in laying blame for the failure of our efforts to eradicate Pontsho's affliction. Our condemnation was piled on Mapule's mother. Some among us recalled having heard rumours of her selling her retarded daughter's womanhood to supplement her meagre pension. Some recalled earlier stories that the daughter was the offspring of the mother's incestuous relationship with her own brother. That was said to have happened after the death of her husband a few months after the marriage.

It was bound to happen. Those of us who understood Pontsho's attitude knew that she would lose patience with our interference in her palm and its omen. She berated us, told us to go swap our trousers for skirts; as she put it, real men would find worthier employment for their time than counting goat and chicken droppings. Really, was respect for one's elders, and male ones for that matter, so reduced that unmarried girls could allude to our manhood in public? We knew then that man's dignity was eroded.

Later, we wished we had taken more offence; that would have confirmed we still took pride in being men. But it was like she had cast a spell over us. Some said all who stood close enough to her to inhale the smell of her armpits behaved strangely afterwards. One old man went even further: he said the eyes of those who had crossed her path or touched her during her menstrual period were forever glazed – immune to any sight except her. Were it not for his age, we were certain the younger men who were constantly wooing Pontsho would have burned him alive. For his insinuation was that their potential bride was a witch. What they did not know, though, was that Pontsho would one day marry death.

The saga of Pontsho's affliction culminated when she received a letter from her twin brother. The one known to have died at the age of twelve in a fall from his bicycle. How strange things were becoming these days. When we were growing boys, we would fall from tall trees, bruising our knees or breaking the occasional rib, finger, leg or arm. But really! To die of a fall from something that creeps on the ground – what punishment were the ancestors meting out, and for what?

That letter certainly had an impact on Pontsho, and on all of us. We once again converged on her compound. We trampled and crushed each other as we vied to see, touch and smell the envelope from the dead, because Pontsho refused to let us see the contents of the letter itself. Each of us scrutinised and sniffed it for signs or proof that it was indeed from the beyond.

'Say, how much postage stamp did it cost?'

'Did it take two months to deliver, like other letters?'

'I don't know... I don't know,' Pontsho mumbled.

'Was it an owl, a white chicken or goat that delivered it?'

'Does he say if there is abundant beer, meat and shade?

These were some of the questions that Pontsho had to deal with. We salivated as we echoed the last question. But Pontsho spoiled our longing for the other world by mumbling, 'I know nothing... I know nothing.'

Poor Pontsho. It was the first time we'd seen her tongue-tied and speechless. Her eyes darting about, appealing, searching for volunteers to provide answers.

'What does he say... what does he want?' in one collective voice we asked.

She just looked at us and hid her face in her palms, as if in prayer.

'Hahaa! A reye, go on, find a way to ridicule her for this as well,' we secretly intoned, passing around the yellow, soil-stained envelope.

Some of the womenfolk tried to soothe Pontsho: 'Relax Pontsho, it is probably one of your suitors playing tricks on you.'

'Patience, the drunkard behind all this will emerge.'

'It's just pranks by that besotted Tumpus.'

But Pontsho started crying, ranting and tearing at her clothes. Oh! Such a beauty gone mad, what a waste of human art, what a waste of fine wife material – so thought the men, both young and old. For them, it meant losing a potential first, second or even third wife. But no, it was not yet time for jealous spinsters and witches to celebrate, for Pontsho stopped her wild behaviour. She gathered herself, went into one of the huts and collected a hoe, a gourd of beer, some one-cent coins, two candles and a plate. Then we knew where she was going. We followed her at a distance as she made her hasty way to the cemetery.

It was only at the cemetery gates that we stopped her. Sounds of a cock crowing from the village could be heard. We reminded her it was taboo to enter graveyards during daytime, except for burials.

'You can't, Pontsho; you can't tend your brother's grave at this time. That will bring bad luck. You have to go before sunrise,' Mme-Makgatho told her.

We heard the distant cock crowing again. Without arguing, Pontsho let herself be led back to her compound by the old woman. Our procession followed at a safe distance. When the crowing came the third time, we could only wonder who was being betrayed this time.

It was noticed by all that the letter incident marked the final transformation of Pontsho. While she did not go out of her way to be polite, she stopped mocking us. As if in reaction to this, our banter, jokes and marathon beer-drinking sessions lost their momentum. It was like the whole village was suffering from a virus of anti-humour.

Unlike normally, when our ears would quickly pick up and interpret the whisperings of the wind, it took us a whole four months to get the information regarding the contents of Pontsho's letter from her late twin brother. That those sketchy dribs and drabs came through Mapule, Mme-Makgatho's retarded daughter, irritated us the most. Did Pontsho have to stoop that low to show her contempt for us, by confiding in a dribbling and drooling human waste? That made us swallow our pride. We reluctantly also found ourselves forced to censor those who still persisted in ridiculing the retarded girl.

One Wednesday morning, the retarded girl surprised us by informing us that we should prepare for Pontsho's betrothal party. The village entered a period of pandemonium: most men neglected kgotla and village council affairs to busy themselves with sorting cattle, goats and hens for possible lobola. But then the retarded girl infuriated us by telling us that none of us, despite our vast wealth, were a match for Pontsho's husband-to-be.

'What pomposity!'

'What a presumptuous insult!'

'What disrespectful gibberish!'

The words floated around us.

'What upstart is this?'

'From whose womb did he come?'

By then, we were convinced that the upstart was not from our village. No, he was certainly not.

Because all the young men had turned to accusing us of stealing their bride, while we in turn had been pointing crooked forefingers at them. Most had ducked or hidden behind tree trunks and stumps, for they feared bad luck would strike them from our spite- and muti-imbued fingers.

This time around, chewing our beards did not offer any comfort. How could it, when we were robbed of a young thoroughbred – a mount to rejuvenate our blood flow?

'Fragile old beards cannot replace brooms to clear our soiled huts. Why, then, do old and young poke each other's eyes with dirty fingernails? Pontsho belongs to the ones that reside in the shades...'

We all turned, mouths and eyes wide open, palms glued to our cheeks as we listened to the retarded Mapule. Gathering ourselves, we hastily pulled away from the girl. Then, like chastised children, we huddled together.

'Cry for yourselves, lost men. In your prime, armed with impatience, you charged forward to find infancy in old age. Retreating, you will find infancy in childhood... Pontsho is loved by spirits whose shadows are mist...'

That finally convinced us that Mapule, apart from being retarded, was in fact mad. Young men jumped forward and started tying her up with ropes. Dead tree-trunks and logs were hastily brought and a bonfire made. We retreated, and had to cover our noses as the burning witch filled the air with nauseating odour.

Days after the roasting, we went about comforting each other. 'Yaa! I've always warned you that Pontsho's conduct was that of one bewitched. But who would have known that the witch was a retarded girl?' one old man said, repeatedly stroking his beard.

'Indeed… indeed, your words strike the very tip of the cow's horns. What can we say?' another added.

In former times, those words would have been downed with nicely brewed sorghum or marula beer. But not today, or for a couple days after the frying. Our stomachs could not retain anything.

Early one morning, not long after Mapule's death, Pontsho once again collected snuff, sorghum beer and grave-cleaning tools and left for the graveyard. And that was the last time we ever saw her. Rumour would later reach us that she had eloped with this or that old or young man, but those men would spend days thereafter cursing and wishing that our accusations were true. Another rumour was that she had dug open her brother's grave.

'Aowa, lena. Then how did she manage to refill the grave?'

Almost thirty years have passed since Pontsho's affliction, but the village hasn't forgotten it. Maybe it is because, here in the village, time hobbles along like old men and women, whose spouses are the marula and mokgope beers that caress their gullets and soothe their old-age loneliness.

Our grandchildren feel it is their duty to offer constant reminders of the incident in their games. They invented a new game called 'greet-scratch'; the playing entails pretending to meet for the first time. Two children extend their hands as if to shake, as is customary; and that is where the climax of the game comes. Just before clasping, each pretends his or her hand is itching, and starts scratching vigorously, first with the fingers of the same hand, then with the other. Then both pretend surprise to see each other thus engaged in scratching.

'Mokgotsi! What is poverty doing to me, me? Receive money – hao! batho, are the ancestors mocking my suffering?'

Or, 'O ra nna, everything repossessed, including relatives and friends. But who is it that will shake my hand in greeting? A re itse, maybe the cold-and-bones palms of the dead?'

The children then laugh so heartily that some roll on the gravel.

A SOOTHSAYER'S DEPOSIT

'Ousie, hey! Ousie, give ten rands and I will tell your future,' the malnourished stranger said to Karabo.

'That's too cheap, hee?'

'What...?' he stammered, his eyes shifting from the hem of her skirt to her handbag. A potential bag-snatcher or serial-killer, she concluded.

'Such a cheap future doesn't need any telling,' she snapped, walking on.

'Please, ousie, I'm serious. Listen, I see you touting a vase. The vase for sale is filled with your future husband's blood,' he whispered, sauntering behind her, his right hand extended to receive payment.

'Uu! Shame. Try somebody else. If I were you, I would concentrate more on seeing employment opportunities in my own future.' Karabo was amused by her own response to the hustler. That's what he was, a deceptive rogue and a parasite.

What do you expect, with so much unemployment and hunger around? Conniving charlatans were hard at their trade.

Later, when she remembered the prediction, she was really infuriated. How could that demented bastard tell such a lie about her? About Karabo, the groomed and cultured daughter of Rre Thekiso and Mme Kagiso Makgatho.

'Ka mma ruri! A twisted upbringing does indeed affect the brain.'

She realised it was one's moral duty to sympathise with such souls, reduced to roguery by poverty. But nonetheless, in the days that followed, her indignation grew. She went out into the streets in search of what she now referred to as 'her charlatan', to give him a dressing-down.

Her friends advised her that that wouldn't be enough: 'Take the bastard to court. Sue him.'

'My dear, your humility is scandalous. You should be more assertive. None of us can stand these cheap, lying bastards.'

'A lazy one too.'

'If he were driving a Merc, I mean that would be understandable,' another friend added with bravado.

Her search for her bastard in the streets proved unsuccessful.

'Mogotsi! Set a private detective onto him. I tell you, we shouldn't let him get away with it.'

To Karabo, the suggestion that she hire a contract killer was an insult. 'Me! Put a deposit on another human being's life? What nonsense.' She abhorred violence – so much so that she cursed people who killed rats and mice, be it with poisonous bait or mouse traps, or who trampled on ants and took swipes at flies. She even began to use a catapult with pebbles against beggars who crushed fleas and bugs.

That was twelve years ago.

The riddle intensifies. Chris had come into her life while she was still in mourning. Eight months earlier, her lover, Tiro, had died in a car-hijacking incident. Of the three who were in the car, only her little boy had survived.

Now and then, Karabo would chastise herself... those vile thoughts. What was their source? Why did she at times wish her little son had perished with the others?

His nightmares and piercing screams. Every Friday towards dawn, he would repeat the same word: '*Nooooooooooooo...!*' But even in his sleep, he could not bring himself to finish his plea: 'Don't kill my father.' And she would cuddle him, her tears mingling with his sweat. Which together seeped down like Tiro's blood, oozing out with his life.

'Your child is haunted,' a sangoma told her family and the late Tiro's when they went to inquire about the boy's disturbed state.

'That's rubbish! Our son was a Christian,' Tiro's mother snapped. What sacrilege! Dead Christians don't roam about haunting the living – and that was the sangoma's insinuation.

'Aowa Mma...' the sangoma began to plead with Tiro's mother.

'Listen! Even if he never burned candles in church at Easter, that doesn't mean that he was not committed,' the furious mother continued.

After protracted arguing along these lines, the sangoma was forced to clarify his statement: 'The child is haunted by fear. Fear that all male figures in his life will be killed in hijack incidents.'

Tiro's mother was calmed, and grudgingly accepted this explanation.

It was only later, when she was alone, that the sangoma's warning struck Karabo as peculiar. She regretted not having challenged him to clarify his divination there and then. Then she would not have this inner torment... worrying is addictive, like a drug.

Because she was preoccupied with raising her son, she never had the time to ponder the possibility of a thread between the sangoma's words and the soothsayer's prediction. She saw life as a bed, a smooth bed on which you stretch yourself out to enjoy a good night's sleep. At times you really enjoy it, while at other times it feels like gravel particles have crawled into your sheets, and during your sleep proceed to scratch your skin, kneading it roughly, so that you wake up with tiny pains and pricks. Sometimes, nightmares creep into your sleep like the nimble fingers of pick-pockets, and you wake up with the nagging feeling that all was not well in your sleep. Or, worse still, nightmares like a stampede of buffaloes storm into your solitude, and you jerk from your bed screaming.

If life was like that, especially if you were Karabo, what would you do? You would simply soldier on, carrying on with the business of getting the best out of life and dumping the bothersome rest into the nearest dustbin.

That was seven years ago.

From the outset, when he came into her life, Karabo was convinced Chris was her God-chosen partner. That is, after Tiro. Now and then, in fact frequently, a bodiless male voice would urge her to embrace him with all her heart. With time, she started associating that voice with Tiro. It appeared that Chris had been hand-picked by her late fiancé to partner her in shouldering the toils of life.

Chris was her opposite. To him, life was a menu of repulsive dishes, maybe with an occasional serving of finer desserts. But the rest... 'I swear, it is horrible. This is the explanation for degrading, trivial human ailments like running stomachs, running noses, headaches and so on... they might appear minor irritations, but they are permanent reminders of our mortality.' (In this, Chris was in fact paraphrasing the farewell statement of Queen Mamahlola on her death-bed in 1903.)

Yet, despite this disadvantage, as Karabo termed his negative philosophy of life, Chris had the potential to be a fine husband.

The noose. Though she didn't believe in fortune-tellers, sangomas and others who tamper with the future or the supernatural, Karabo was increasingly becoming convinced that the dead could, and do, engage in dialogue with the living. Certainly, Tiro was busy grooming Chris as his successor in her affections. Having reached this conclusion, her mood was celebratory. But all she managed was to have an unpleasant dream.

Her dream was on an intriguing encounter with a man from up north. He telephoned to inform her that he had stolen her husband's manhood. He offered to restore the stolen potency on condition she consented to sleep with him: 'Yebo Mkhatsi, wena shleep wid me. Mi give bag yoou husiband's shing.'

It was an unsavoury bargain.

'Never! That you will never get. You filthy scoundrel. I would rather give whatever ransom you demand. Anything but that.'

And what was anything? Anything was anything. 'I am prepared for whatever to save my potential marriage.'

The dream could have continued, except that in trying to grab the man by the scruff of his neck and wring it, she fell from the sofa. Karabo sighed with relief.

Her relief was short-lived though. The noose tightened. The dream's spell was not broken. She had to conquer her enemy in dreams for it to translate into reality. A vicious circle.

Another source of relief was that she had a child – comfort in itself, definite proof of her fertility. A child, a boy: triumphant testimony of her loins.

The dead... when they speak, they say, 'Habahabahaba,' or mumble similar unfamiliar sounds. It is a cryptic language very few people can understand. Maybe that is why diviners and spirit mediums are needed. To decode that ethereal talk. It was because of this that Karabo resolved to consult a spirit medium. To inquire with the dead about the soothsayer's prediction. Illusions do bring comfort at times. People like to be told that they will live to a thousand years, or that in their next life they'll be reincarnated as billionaires. Karabo was no exception.

The spirit medium took her into a future of fascinations, a future infested with brothels selling private parts for sex-change operations, restaurants and take-aways serving streaming human blood, butcheries offering lay-bye purchase on human embryos, sperm and ovaries. Twists in the labyrinth.

That future held everything except what she wanted to know – how could she, Karabo, a God-fearing Christian, hire killers to take her future husband's life? For this is how she understood the medium's words. More twists in the labyrinth.

Resolved to find the answer, she decided to consult another spirit medium. He was sympathetic to her situation, but like Alexander the Great's sorcerer, he demanded she present jewellery to unseal the lips of the dead.

They could be exorbitant, the dead, she cursed. To think that during their time they may have subsisted on a couple of cattle and goats, and prided themselves on being frugal. And their agents – fortune-tellers, sangomas and spirit mediums, and a few charlatans – seemed resolved to undo that injustice by living in opulence.

She was far, far better, the third spirit medium. Like all such people, she first took Karabo on a detour. She led her through a future where nursery schools offered tuition in pick-pocketing, bag-snatching and other petty crimes; a tomorrow in which lower grades offered courses in car-hijacking, kidnapping and extortion. She shrieked, sneezed and belched repeatedly. And uttered the damning warning that the Four Horsemen of the Apocalypse were frantic, grooming and harnessing their wild stallions, sharpening their swords, preparing for the final battle. It was then that Karabo felt convinced that her Chris would not survive… that she was fated to lose another man. She thought of Lot's wife, turned into a pillar of salt. Her destiny was dim, cursed and sealed, like Jocasta's or Medea's.

Unless…

That was five years ago.

Karabo grew up in the faith that good does triumph over evil. Or is supposed to. It was because of this that she prepared herself to beat the bad omens. She started giving more alms to the poor. She reasoned that if beggars could sustain themselves, the whole economic equation would be balanced. Secure people wouldn't harass the pavements for coins.

Like pigeons gathering around their feeders at Joubert Park, legions of beggars would swarm around her, pecking and nibbling at pennies. To keep them nourished, she started growing coins in her pockets, purse and parcels. This didn't worry her bankers: 'Never mind the young lady, our vaults can hardly cope with all those coins. Let her take them.' But they became alarmed when she started drawing from her retirement and pension investments.

> *Beggars and muggers, beggars and muggers*
> *give me beggars and muggers*
> *give me one, two, three coins*

beggars and muggers, beggars and muggers
round the corner, somewhere
round that alley, one, two, three
give me beggars and muggers...

Karabo had a harmonious voice. She would whistle as she sat feeding the assembled beggars. All who heard the refrain would unconsciously start repeating it. Including beggars and muggers. Within a short time, it hit the charts of local radio and television stations. It was no surprise when, months later, it topped the Billboard Charts. *Beggars and muggers...*

The beggar is king of the concrete jungle, ruthlessly preying for coins; muggers come afterwards to scrape for leftovers. Karabo rationalised that, with the removal of beggars, society's cancer would be cured. Then vicious species like car-hijackers wouldn't endanger her Chris.

With time, she realised how pathetic her spirit medium's diatribes, as she now termed them, were. Had she, the spirit medium, any decency, she would throw her necromancy into the sewers where it belonged.

But Chris threw her back into confusion by winning a 5-Series BMW in a charity competition. He further earned her ire by insisting on keeping it.

'Please, darling, sell it… swap it for money instead, please. Anything but that car. I don't want the whole township queuing to rob us,' she pleaded with him.

'C'mon, dear.' She so hated it when he put on that American accent. 'You can't be serious, Karabo. You really mean we give away a gift from the ancestors?'

'Please, dear, for my sake…'

'What about their sake?'

'*Chris!*' she stopped immediately, shock on her face. Was it really her, screaming at her husband? 'I'm sorry, Chris, I didn't mean to shout. But you know the danger such things expose us to.'

'They gave it as a present. They will probably look after it.'

'But Chris, are you serious? Car-hijackers are everywhere, whereas your ancestors are long rotten down below…'

For the first time, Chris hit her. She was so stunned that she could not bring herself to speak to him for several weeks.

In his naïveté, like most men, he was convinced it was out of anger or because she begrudged his infringing on her freedom of expression. He pleaded that he would never hurt her again. He vowed that he would do anything to please her, even forfeit his right to life to make amends with his angel. His repentance touched her, but she could not utter a word to him for days; such humility and remorse left her speechless. Throughout that period, he maintained his vigil of coming to kneel before her, entreating her to have mercy on her chastised little devil. But he kept the car all the same. That was a year ago.

She started having frequent dreams of him driving in a brakeless car. The precipice edge. Sometimes the car would topple over a cliff, at times it would plunge into a speeding train at a level crossing; sometimes, like a powerboat, it would streak over water. It wouldn't stop at robots. Without consulting any spirit medium, she knew it was a bad omen. The precipice edge again.

She visited a private detective. The detective passed her on to his buddy who sold car security systems. He told her about new advances in technology, the advantages of satellite-tracking devices for cars.

'With those little chips, you would be able to monitor the exact movements of your husband.'

'Don't misunderstand me. It is not his movements but those of his car that I am interested in.'

'Come now, lady, don't be shy or guilty about it. It is common these days for spouses to spy on each other. Who can blame them, with so much unfaithfulness going around? Add the high tax levies on single and divorced parties, it is only reasonable that we all take precautions.'

'My husband is not that type – the divorcing or deserting kind. You see, I need to be on the alert about his security. Sort of install a warning message for him to avoid certain roads. Like a bleeper or a panic-button or some such thing… of course I want it done anonymously. I mean it must sound like… you know, like the traffic report. But this one should advise against using certain routes because of hijacking dangers.'

'Lady, I don't know what you're talking about. You're looking for some high-tech James Bond type gadget. Are you in the espionage profession or what?'

'Look! Can you install it or not? And for how much?'

'I certainly can. But unfortunately, we don't have such a gadget at the moment. Come and inquire after a decade, say. Hey, in the meantime, talk it over with your neighbourhood watch.'

Sarcasm in such bad taste was infuriating to Karabo, especially by groomed salespeople who joke about everything.

Having considered the matter for some months, Karabo found she couldn't bear to sit idly by and wait, so she revisited the salesman, that crusader of merriment and good cheer, to sign the contract for a custom-made device. The device was highly rated, supposedly only in use by the CIA. Because of that, the crusader demanded a hundred-thousand-rand advance payment.

'Christ! Where do I get such money?'

'How much is a human life, tell me, lady? How much would you say your spouse is worth?'

'It's not how much he's worth. You've already put a price on him.'

'Come on, lady. It is an arbitrary number. I could have said a hundred rand. You most certainly would have felt insulted then.'

'I just can't afford such money right away…'

'Put a deposit then. A couple of thousands now, say ten, and the rest later. How's that, hmm?

I see relief in your face, hmm! I'll be damned if we don't have a deal.'

That Friday dawn her son didn't scream, and Karabo had one of the longest and most relaxing sleeps she'd ever had.

WHEN A NAME AWAKES

Though he looked forty, Tutankhamen was in fact thirty. He had a slight stoop, bowed legs and a hardened face, a mask of wrinkles and furrows. What interested me, though, was not the face. In our part of the world, there are many faces like his – faces defaced by suffering, distorted by the merciless hand of hard labour, faces on which the tortures of life have been drawn. In some, the loss of loved ones is written in their eyes: the loss of children, of friends. Because there is no more room in their hearts to hide and harbour it, the pain seeps out and ends up etching its hideous signature on their faces. In a way, Tutankhamen's face was like those crumbled facades, on which nature has chosen to paint its saddest murals. Murals that compliment those painted by the political masters of our land in the early sixties.

But what interested me, and others, about him was that precious yet dispensable thing we call a name. There was much speculation about its origin. On several occasions, he'd been asked about his hereditary name — the sacred one that is passed from one generation to another, serving as a link, or proof of one's allegiance to tradition. The one that is usually accompanied by totems and praise poems.

Tutankhamen told me his family were descendants of the great Khazimola. Then he looked at me sternly, maybe because he thought I would chuckle or giggle, as most people did. But I couldn't. I could not laugh at the bearer of the name while that tormented face was staring at me.

Old rumour had it that Khazimola, meaning 'the one who always yawns', got the name because his every emotion was expressed in yawning. He was known to spend days without uttering a word. His wives were always keen to give testimony to that. His drinking friends also attested to the fact that he could share calabashes of beer for hours on end without laughing, even at the most amusing jokes. It was also said that he was incapable of shedding tears, even on the tragic loss of four of his five wives. Then there was the death of seven of his children. Again, that did not induce his tear ducts to relent and show his humanity.

A seven-year drought followed. Everybody, including the chief, was desperate. Khazimola's only reaction during those days was said to be fits of yawning. Then the chief's only son and heir died. Khazimola would have yawned as well, except that, as the village's chief muti-man, his honour and wisdom were now questioned.

Then he wept, a seven-day wail that is said to have disturbed the repose of the ancestors. After that, he was given a new name, Nyembezi. He could not bear the ridicule of that name – the wailer, the lamenter, the teary one – and he opted to do what all disgraced men do. He took a mixture made of a crocodile's brain.

The village entered a period of renewal as they went about initiating their new chief muti-man. A few tears were shed in mourning for Khazimola, but everybody knew it was an empty ceremony, bidding farewell to an unlamented failure. For how could a great muti-man, as Khazimola, later Nyembezi, have failed to protect and shield the chief's son?

That is how the Khazimolas ended up being called the Nyembezis. The family had to live with the new name, which served as a reminder of their fall from grace. That was until Tutankhamen's grandfather returned from the Great War, having been in one of the few black platoons that had faced and survived 'Mjeremane'. It was there, in the vast desert, that Tutankhamen's grandfather first heard about the mummified Egyptian pharaohs. His fascination with them was great. He asked and gathered information about them. And he vowed that, should he survive Mjeremane's fierce bullets, he would erase his family's imposed servility and restore it to greatness again.

On his return from the war, he was one of the few local heroes. He was held in high esteem. Crowds used to hang around him as he narrated his adventures. Everybody was awed and fascinated when he talked of the great dry land where sand and sky embrace; where wind-storms and heat are partners that squash man between them. With time, his stories became longer and more varied, but none could argue with him. For in the village, most men had chosen to hide in the caves and mountains rather than answer the call to go fight the great witch-doctor from the north.

That is how that noble name, Tutankhamen, took root at the foot of the Hlabati Mountains. Until the second-generation Tutankhamen choose to profane it, thirty years later in Alexandra. Tutankhamen was to blame for this. But then, the time and world he lived in wasn't that innocent either. Had he been someone else, he would have led a happy life. But Tutankhamen choose to be ambitious in a land where ambition for people of a darker skin was sacrilege.

There were many times he wished that the gods had endowed him with a lighter skin. A skin that would have ensured him the warmest rays of sun in winter, the coolest shade in the harsh summer. He'd grown up hearing stories of Santa Claus, who distributed beautiful goods not only in white households, but in their dustbins as well.

That he was one of only two surviving members of the 1959 Sub A class at Ikageng Primary School was achievement enough. But he made the terrible mistake of thinking that all men were equal. He thought that because all have incubated in a woman's womb for the same duration of time, and sucked from a breast where warmth and tenderness flows, that all would be warm and tender towards each other. But no; the warmth and tenderness nurtured in human beings from conception onwards is soon wiped away by greed and ambition. Wasn't that the reason he and his older brother were now estranged? There was bitter rivalry to inherit their late father's possessions.

Or was it because those who start kicking violently while still in the womb, or those who take savage bites at their mother's tits while sucking, are destined to be equally savage in later life?

It didn't take long before the rumour started circulating that Tutankhamen was a direct descendant of the great pharaoh himself. The drunkards at the shebeen argued about it: 'You are a liar!'

'Hey! Mamela… why do people always name their children after somebody else in the family? Usually somebody late. Hee! Tell me?'

'Life is a circle. We sleep in death and awake again in birth. Fools! Can't you see, the great man himself is back.'

'Liar! Where is your kingdom?'

'Hey! Kgosi, re botse, where are your subjects?'

'Ba-gaetsho! Tlang le bone se-tsoga bahung, Kgosi Tutankhamen.' People joked and laughed.

However, Tutankhamen's life did not change. Instead, he plunged deeper into his suffering. Fleeing that, and the inhumanity of his countrymen, he found solace in the bottle. He embraced and wrapped his solitude in its acids. It was only when boasting about being the reincarnation of Tutankhamen that his sense of self-worth was restored. And he relentlessly peddled that story.

Township gossip-mongers gave the story wings to fly. In their re-telling, new narrators added new plots to rescue the story from becoming a cliché. These stories started reaching Tutankhamen at his different drinking spots. He would roar with laughter, buy beers and offer toasts to the narrators.

Soon the story became known throughout Alexandra, from First to Twenty-second Avenue. It spilled over and was recounted at garden parties in the East Bank. Then it invaded Lombardy East. New settlers from Alexandra related it to their white neighbours across pre-cast fences. Inquisitive children built platforms next to the fences to hear their elders better. Eager dogs burrowed and dug fervently, collapsing the walls. Most people thought they were after treasured bones, but it soon became clear they were pioneers in destroying divisions between neighbours.

Youngsters from Lombardy East started relating the story to their school classmates from other suburbs. Soon it spread to Linksfield and Fourways. Innovative essays that surprised English masters with their poignancy followed.

'Huwiii! Tutankhamen in Alexandra, hahaa! What a joke! Of all places.'

'But dear, they say it is true. Several newspapers are said to have assigned their investigative reporters to look into the rumour...'

'Huwii! What a waste, kana those illiterates like exaggerating their worth. And for newspapers to buy such rubbish!'

It wasn't long before a local newspaper ran a front-page teaser:

HOAX OR EIGHTH WONDER?

*Alex man claims to be reincarnation
of Pharaoh Tutankhamen.*

Page 2

'Shame! Unscrupulous reporters out for a cheap scoop,' said the editor of a rival newspaper. But then he, too, saw fit to send his chief reporter to investigate the rumour. And Tutankhamen found himself enjoying some measure of the good life. He was wined, dined and chauffeured around by different newspapers, each determined to out-bid the other for an exclusive interview.

This was one of the major reasons why he believed he was superior to Rambane. The latter was the only other surviving member of the 1959 Sub A class.

'O-hwoo! don't bother to mention that one. The alcoholic, the hobo, the idiot,' Tutankhamen would say dismissively whenever people mentioned his former buddy. 'Who? Rambane, e'sbotho leso.'

Still, between them there wasn't much of a difference.

'Of course there is,' one of Tutenkhamen's drinking companions might say. 'Rambane has never had his picture in the newspapers…'

'Except that time when he appeared in the Community News section – for relatives to come identify a near-frozen hobo found in a donga.'

This was despite Rambane having once challenged members of the Young Ones gangsters after the kidnapping of his younger sister and girlfriend. And despite him telling the story over and over, and storming the local newspaper and insisting that they publish it. His audience would always ignore his animated gesticulations, frothings and swearings. The worst was when they dismissed his offer of money. He realised that prosperity has destroyed humanity, when time-honoured gestures like honoraria were so easily dismissed.

Tutankhamen started telling everybody that a large reward was coming his way. He would contentedly stoke his beard and rub his belly. He also added that he was going to marry Sis Phuti. Everybody envied him, for Sis Phuti was one of the elegant beauties on the shebeen circuit. The stories reached Sis Phuti. She stopped going to shebeens with us. Her face lost some of its furrows. Even the bitterness around her mouth disappeared. A swagger replaced her habitual dragging gait. Her female friends said she was grooming herself for a life in the East Bank or Lombardy East, where the couple was naturally expected to live. She was also said to spend most of her Friday and Saturday nights practising new drinking manners: the delicacy that was reputed to go with wine sipping, the tilting of the head when talking, the throwing back of the neck, thrusting out of the bosom and gentle flapping of the hands when chatting and laughing with important people.

With concealed envy for both of them — and openly expressed congratulations — we waited for the cash reward to be delivered. After months of patient waiting, it became clear that somebody's tongue had slipped terribly. Word was that Sis Phuti now frequented little-known, remote shebeens. It was said she only stayed for brief moments.

By the time we caught up with her, it was three months later. During which period Tutankhamen had grown a distinct stoop. He was said to be heavily weighed down by Sis Phuti's abuse and insults. I was there when she finally slapped and ridiculed him publicly.

'S'botho tena! Hhmmm? Am I cheap, hmm? Where is your Lombardy East? Sis! Nja ena. Futsek! With your cheap beers... cheap babalaas... cheap, smelly socks... Se-azi abanqono thena. Not cheap dogs. Smelly underwear – sis! Smelly armpits.'

In stunned silence, we watched. Despite the effect of the beer in our heads, the lessons of our elders held firm: never ever interfere in the affairs of a man and his woman. Never! That is why we had always viewed marriage counsellors as idling meddlers.

Then I saw Tutankhamen's wrinkles and furrows draw tighter under the weight of that silence. Sis Phuti stood up, walked up to Tutankhamen, spat in his face and walked out. Everybody knew she was gone for good.

'It's true... ka rre! the newspapers said so. Please call her back. It's true, my brother is gone. I am the sole survivor to inherit my grandfather's pension,' he kept on repeating.

At four in the morning, when I left the shebeen, he was still wailing his misfortunes.

ARUNAH'S JIGSAW PUZZLE

SHE,
Arunah, will emerge
bearing the universe on her shoulders,
sampling tomorrows
arranged like her plaited hair…

ARUNAH WAS A COMPULSIVE jigsaw puzzle builder. 'Addict' might be an appropriate term. Her twenty-fifth birthday would be in 1997. As a mother, I was confident of my predictions of good fortune for her. I was certain that my schemes for her future would be successful and that her life, that revered jigsaw puzzle, would fit one piece into another.

A jigsaw puzzle was the only heirloom bestowed upon her, despite being the cause of heated and ugly quarrels between her father and I.

'You! Let the child play with dolls like any other normal girl,' my husband used to rant.

'Not my special child,' I would respond.

But later on, I would only mumble the words. Who wouldn't, with those terrible beatings I used to receive? All this despite Thabiso's pretences of being a gentleman – that was the image he projected to the world, to friends, lovers and strangers. He had the enviable status in the township of being one of the few town council clerks who possessed a standard eight certificate.

Yet in the end, as always, womanly will-power prevailed, and Arunah was permitted to play with her jigsaw puzzle whenever she wished.

My suspicions that the puzzle was becoming an increasingly life-distorting feature were confirmed by the time of Arunah's sixteenth birthday. With apprehension, anxiety and hope, I waited and watched for her to start showing an interest in boys. Anxiety changed to panic when I discovered that she was not even menstruating.

Visits to different gynaecologists followed – at first reluctant forays, later on in desperate hysteria. Then to urologists. And all concluded and confirmed: 'There is nothing wrong with the physical features of your daughter, ma'am.'

Then those doctors gave way to psychiatrists. Spurred on by the haranguing of relatives, we ended up consulting sangomas and Zionist prophets.

By then, Arunah was eighteen.

All my paranoia, self-blame and panic went unappreciated. For despite all my trials, Arunah remained calm and unperturbed. She blossomed and gained that oily radiance of the celibate.

It was then that legions of young men started patrolling our street. Some settled down opposite our gate, opting to wait. Some even recruited the neighbourhood kids to maintain surveillance of her movements. Our block became a hive of activity: cheerful young men full of confidence; jerky, nervous boys with unsteady eyes; ridiculous, bald-headed, pot-bellied local businessmen; those skinny, snot-sucking young taxi-drivers. Not to be left out of the snare were young sergeants, detectives and even informers. The labyrinth set to weaving itself into an all-consuming black hole.

My motherly anxieties were left suspended on a tightrope. Each morning, the rays of the sun fuelled and fed the emotional inferno raging within me. 'Badimo! Nthuseng maimeng akhuii!' I ended up lamenting. The hope that my daughter was becoming normal was gradually confirmed. But oh! The consequences!

One afternoon, spying from behind my curtains, I saw them. That they liked each other was apparent in the way she beamed and kept turning shyly aside, and the way his eyes radiated. Then I saw him taking her hand and edging closer. My heartbeat quickened.

Then Arunah was nineteen…

> *She would*
> *rave, scribble and unscramble words,*
> *works and rites deformed by*
> *metaphoric speeches…*

One night I was awakened by mournful wailings. It turned out to be our neighbour's four dogs. An owl then decided to add its hooting to the chorus. Fearful, I tiptoed to my daughter's bedroom. I found her sitting on her bed, looking through the east-facing window that overlooked East Bank and Lombardy East.

My mind immediately set to work to unravel the meaning of her behaviour. No matter what, I had to come to the conclusion that that all would be right in the end. I quickly and quietly started fitting the jigsaw pieces together. 'I see!… Her young man must be living in East Bank, probably from some well-to-do family, hmmmm!' I proudly decided.

But it was immediately after that incident that the nagging feelings that Arunah was relapsing into her strange world started resurfacing. She now preferred the company of female dolls. Dumb lifeless dolls! Little white-people dolls, because then black dolls were rare. And she would spend hours on end with them.

Hopelessly, I realised that, even at that age, she persisted with her childhood fantasy of growing up to be white. I couldn't stand the thought of psychologists and herbal-healers' consultation fees – again!

My only comfort was that she had not yet seemed to notice that the real jigsaw puzzle, her own life, was not fitting into a single integrated picture. She continued with her devoted task of putting the puzzle together, convinced that she was fashioning a classical masterpiece. But it was a sketch shaped with brush strokes of make-believe and wishes. In reality, it could not fit together, could not make one inspired painting. Nothing that Magandela, Mahlangu or Sekoto would have given a second glance.

I was still absorbed in those thoughts when lingering memory brought back Mrs Rosettenville, the palm-reader and fortune-teller from whom we got warnings about the potent omen of the jigsaw puzzle. Even now, I can still vividly remember our encounter with her. Arunah was still an infant then, and we had just come from seeing Dr Leeuesmann, the paediatrician at 97 Claim Street.

Then I recalled what my grandmother used to say: women are not twin sisters. Each is given according to the dictates of the gods. Even their wombs are not the same or equal. Some give birth to sweety-lovely things that will take care of them in their later years, while others waste their precious nine months carrying little snakes in their wombs. With me – what could I say was my portion?

Some women in the stokvel and manyano hinted that I had given birth to an old princess who was reluctant to accept the fact that she had came back among commoners.

'Mosadi! Had you known... were she mine, I would have wrung her pompous little neck immediately after birth.'

'And then go claim someone else's baby afterwards?'

'Anyway, I don't care much about children. If it wasn't for that stupid Mamazala of mine...'

'Who can listen to you – except those who don't know that you have ten children?'

Then Arunah was twenty.

It was predictable that the words of that fortune-teller would haunt me forever. Every time I think of them, a chilling shiver runs down my spine: 'Her crown will sink in... then it will result in her main palm lines crossing each other, and...' Her next words had been drowned out by the drone of a passing double-decker bus. And despite my pleading, Mrs Rosettenville would not repeat herself. Ever since, I've dreaded touching or looking at my daughter's palms.

It was then not surprising that on her twenty-second birthday I should be obsessed with determining her future. More especially, what she would be at twenty-five. I had all the time then for such leisurely thoughts, with my husband divorced. And the fact that his new wife was a husband-abuser did go some way towards compensating for my punch-bag past with him.

Even my Arunah was gone. She was lost and buried in desperate attempts at solving the jigsaw puzzle – attempts which were increasingly becoming affected by her unpredictable moods. One moment she would be excited and chattering like a well-nourished infant, while the next she would be moaning and swearing like a spoiled brat having her tooth extracted. And between these moods, she was never stable enough to have the patience to fit the little jigsaw puzzle pieces together. There were times when she would literally cry when she failed to fit them.

Some of the pieces could fit interchangeably in various positions. But there were a couple that constituted the core of the jigsaw puzzle, and those could only fit in particular positions. Yet, of late, it seemed they had acquired awkward curves and edges, losing their prime status.

I kept on going back to this thing of mine – having given birth to a reincarnated princess. I talked to my church minister. He reprimanded me, and told me not to let the devil lead me astray. He threatened to excommunicate me should I bring the subject up again. Meanwhile, the women in the manyano advised me to marry her off quickly, with the assertion that once she tasted the pleasures of sex she would be cured. I pondered this for hours, and recalled that women are not twin sisters. So shouldn't I take comfort in what the gods had given me?

In desperation I threw myself into books and articles – anything that dealt with withdrawal, reincarnation and people possessed by spirits. I only stopped reading those after encountering one that offended me terribly. It said people who believed in those things were primitive heathens. The writer attributed such cases to mental retardation.

'No-no! My pretty daughter isn't mentally retarded. I swear. Maybe she is bewitched, that I can believe.'

None of this made my daughter any better. Instead, my frantic impatience grew. I sat engrossed in patching together those little threads that would shape her destiny. And that approaching twenty-fifth birthday worried me, for it was at that same age that my mother, like my grandmother and great-grandmother before her, got married and gave birth to their first child. And incidentally, it was at that same age that I too got married and gave birth to Arunah.

'No-no! My pretty daughter is not retarded. She is normal... she is normal. It is just that she is dealing with her adolescence in a different way.'

Who knows, maybe there was some truth in talk of her being a princess from long ago. With time, I started dreaming a lot about her. She would appear dressed in strange, long gowns, not any style worn these days. Sometimes I thought I heard her screaming: 'Mme, Mme!!… take me home… take me to Arunah.'

Then I would see her wandering by the banks of a great river. Sometimes she would wade in, summoning the courage to swim. Thankfully, the courage never came to fetch her across.

And what was this 'take me to Arunah' thing? Arunah was her Christian name. I recalled that she'd cried continuously during the name-giving ceremony. She'd rejected all the names that we'd come up with. It was only after one of the aunties mentioned the name of one of the Indian nuns at the hospital that she suddenly stopped crying. And all resolved to adopt that name for her.

> *She would*
> *brave the four winds lashing*
> *from tempest's vengeful mouth,*
> *cohabit with Prometheus, and*
> *set to weaving bulrushes by the*
> *Nile until apocalypse comes*
> *to set man free.*

ALLEY-ALLEY, WHERE IS MY LOVER?

THAT WAS THE LAMENT OF ALMOST EVERY girl in our township. Lerato was one of them. She was one of the loners whose potential lover had skipped the country. Hopes of being reunited with him were slim, mainly because those strange lands seemed infatuated with young men from our land. Who could blame them? For those young men were dreamers. They dreamed aloud. Talked confidently about the future, when they would be ministers, deputy-ministers or diplomats. Some were even confident enough to predict that they would be Minister of Finance. And those foreign women would marvel at the prospect of playing personal assistant to their husbands as they signed and balanced treasury cheques.

Lerato knew that in her case the chance of cutting ribbons at official functions was remote. Her only salvation was probably to disappear into exile for a couple of months. Once there, to publicise herself as much as possible. Strive to meet one or two potential ministers-in-waiting. There was also the possibility of changing her surname and accent. With that, she would be assured affluent returnee status.

Her friend, Thandi, was different. She enjoyed the chat of local boys. Sometimes she would drag Lerato out for a stroll: 'Let's go meet the outies, mhlambe unga thola e ou encha.'

And Lerato would reluctantly accompany her. Then they would go around teasing all the boys they met. On those excursions, it was always Thandi who managed to get new telephone numbers and addresses in her diary.

Lerato thought all that was demeaning. She believed in picking potential lovers at decent places. Yet time was running out for her, after she'd failed to meet any at soccer matches and music concerts. What other places were left? There were street corners, shop stoeps and alleys. Those were far safer than venturing into shebeens.

'Would you mind accompanying me to First Avenue?' Thandi asked one day.

'Wena! I'd love to, but isn't it too late?'

'Come on lovey, it's only half past five.'

'Remember, my mother comes back from work at six. And she likes things to be ready.'

'Ashee! Never mind. We will be back then. A little walk might earn somebody a "prospective".'

'Please, Thandi, promise that we will be back by quarter to six.'

They set off. On the way, Thandi continued teasing the boys. 'Hey! look at that one. See the little lips. Not good for delivering a good kiss... Uuuu! What about that one? Small feet. Probably his thing is small as well – I'm sure of it. Won't be able to satisfy you or make a baby.'

'Yoo! Thandi... sis!'

'Do you want to prove it? Hey! Sonny, come here. What is your name?'

'Ke Lesiba ousie.'

'How old are you?'

'Ke na le fourteen, ousie.'

'Have you ever got it?'

'What?'

'A girl – has any woman ever given you?'

'Err... ousie, they refuse.'

'You see, Lerato? Take him and go try it. Hey! Sonny, ousie ona would like to give you.'

'I'm afraid,' said the boy.

Of course the fun continued through the evening. Lerato only managed to be back at home by quarter past twelve. She was in a bad state. Her face was bruised and swollen.

'Where have you been, dear?' her mother asked.

Lerato responded with a blank stare, tears rolling from her eyes. Her mother tried to press for an answer, but couldn't get one.

The friendship between the two girls suffered as well. 'Lovey, come for a walk,' said Thandi several weeks later.

'I'm sorry, I'm too busy.'

'Why, what's wrong with you? By the way, how did it go last time?'

'Thandi, we better not talk about that.'

Meanwhile, Lerato's mother asked herself over and over what had happened to her. She finally came back to Lerato.

'Don't be ashamed, Lerato. Tell me.'

'Mme... I know I shouldn't have gone along with Thandi.'

'Yes, what about her? Tell me everything.'

'We started off at the Red Flame Tavern, then ended up at Mapetla's. She insisted on ordering beers, even though we didn't have any money. She banked on one of the gents there footing our bill. But when none paid... you know...'

'Hmmm! So they moered you?'

'Sort of.'

Then Lerato's longings turned into a dream. And the dream produced a young man. The dream would slip into her sleep at odd times, during the night when she was asleep, and during the day when she was awake. She saw herself in his arms. With the recurrence of the dream, she became familiar with his features. She would be able to pick him out of a crowd with confidence. But suppose the dream did not materialise? Would she have to settle for some lousy loafer?

With time, as the sun rose and set with its relentless, dull regularity, she realised she had to do something. And that meant going out into the streets. She scouted for months. Still, her dream prince refused to appear.

Lerato, in desperation to find and interpret her dream, ended up jolling with different young men. And her mother would always scold her: 'Hey! Ngwanenyana ke wena? Can't kuku eo ya gago stay without boys for a while?' Or: 'Where do you think all that changing of boyfriends like underwear will lead you?'

Her mother's words would strike her whenever she came from seeing one of those boyfriends of hers. For she would always feel dejected and abused by their methods: hurried, ungentle and at times even hostile. And after a couple of minutes, they were exhausted. Their major concern was to dash off should a group approach. Their unwashed mouths couldn't spare any tender words, nor a thank-you kiss for her favour – just an acrid, nauseating smell. That always left her shattered.

On reflection, she concluded that all the sane young men were no more. It was probably true: all potential partners, those who would have staked out a matrimonial future with her, were either married to foreign lands or in foreign graves. What was left? A marauding lot of pick-pockets, rapists, bank robbers and child molesters.

'That's a shame, Lerato. I mean, there must be some exceptions,' her white colleague, also a cashier at Checkers, said.

'You don't know them. The ones around here are only interested in SSBS.'

'Oooooo! What…?'

'It's Sex, Soccer, Beer and Score – robbery.'

That's when the colleague advised her to join dating and singles' clubs. 'Who knows? Maybe you'll meet your ideal man at one of those places.'

After a couple months of trying dating clubs, Lerato gave up. Her colleague advised her to join voluntary organisations. 'You know, sometimes doing all that keeps you preoccupied. You kind of forget the loneliness. And there is a plus – you might meet some really nice gentleman in one of those programmes.'

Again, Lerato endured doing voluntary work for a couple of months. She would always come home dejected.

One evening her mother said, 'Why not visit your friend?'

'I'm fine here, Mme.'

'No, Lerato. It's a sin for one your age to sit brooding every evening like a widow.'

Lerato forced herself to the door. She gave her mother that vacant look of hers. Seconds later, darkness enveloped her.

Aimlessly, she walked the streets. Searching and searching, for what she knew not. Big dogs greeted her with their hollow booming barks: *Bawoo-bawoooooo...!* and the 'brakkies' echoed with shrill voices: *Bao-bao-bao-bao...!* Bats welcomed her with their haunting whistles: *Tswiee-tswiee...*

She turned a corner into an alley adjoining Fifteenth Avenue. She saw a group of four men standing there. Their profiles took on grotesque shapes when she drew closer.

What if she invited one, would the other three force themselves on her? What if they were zombies, or the restless spirits of the Msomi Gang? Still, she resolved to move on, edge forward, one bold step at a time. It was only when she was opposite them that she could take a guess at their age. Men long past their prime and interest in women. Yet that they were men fuelled the flames burning within her heart and loins. She nonetheless resolved to pass them – tired, spent things. Somewhere in the streets and alleys, she was bound to meet someone. Someone younger, eager and willing to get 'it' for free.

Then, twenty metres ahead of her, she saw him. A solitary man in his prime – that she could tell from his firm, confident steps. He had a solid build, was tall and well fed. He walked on, his shoes ruthlessly crushing the gravel. *Ggrin-ggrin, ggrin-ggrin*, they went. No girl ahead or behind him. As he was approaching, her eyes fixed on his silhouetted profile. She dare not remove them, lest he disappear like her dream. A split second, and he would be gone and lost for ever. 'O-tch!' she whispered. He was already one step past her.

'Dumela, Oubutie,' she said, her voice coming out in a choking rasp.

'Hello Ousikie! Saying anything?' He paused and turned to her.

Her panic was mounting. Then she saw his smile, and was reassured. 'Eerr... err... I only was... said... dumela.'

'Come, Ousikie. I see you are not in a hurry, ne.' He came and stood in front of her. She felt her body tense up. He looked at her face for a while. She felt like a commodity, gauged for its value.

He then gently took her hand and led her to a corner of the derelict alley, next to the wall. Unhurriedly he laid her down. Then on the rough and filthy floor the act was done. It left lingering passion in her. The traffic of passing male voices did not unsettle or disturb him. Afterwards, he awarded her with a cuddle and kiss. She stood watching him as with delicate care he dusted his clothing with a white handkerchief.

'Have... er... do you have 'n ousie?... I would like to become your...'

'Err... don't you think that is a bit rushed?'

'But... just now we enjoyed each other. We could continue seeing each other.'

'I don't know. Maybe... okay. Say... let us meet next Thursday. Say around five in the afternoon. Is that okay?'

On Thursday at four o'clock, Lerato was already prepared. Waiting for him and trying to visualise him. Hopefully he didn't sport knife scars and the like. She wondered what kind of dreams haunted his sleep. Did he see himself like the other dreamers? Or were his dreams flooded with stolen cars fleeing from yellow, white and blue Monza squad cars, flashing blue lights?

While still preoccupied with those thoughts, she saw him coming. He was young and cheerful, full of the energy he'd displayed on the night of their first encounter.

As he moved closer, she could feel her body respond; a burning surge emanating from her loins. His eyes were fixed on her. Stripping her naked with longing and lust. Three steps from her... two... one...

He turned his head away and passed her.

She was stunned. How could he behave like that? The son of a bitch... the shameless piece of donkey dung... the sperm-filled skull! It was only when she paused to think of worse and more befitting curses to heap on him that she realised he wasn't her alley partner.

She bowed her head. When she raised it again, it was five-thirty. She looked around. The township streets were drying up. Stretching themselves for a temporary rest, that is until young lovers invaded them. Her mother was probably already home preparing supper.

Lerato sat waiting. Her head sank down on her breast, tears streaming down her cheeks. She didn't care anymore whether he came or not. She didn't care about anything. When she raised her head again, it was already ten at night. She tried to raise herself, but couldn't. Her head sank forward again. The dogs quietened down. Sounds of speeding cars faded forever.

The following dawn, at four o'clock, the early risers and workers passed her, still in that posture.

LESIBA THE CALLIGRAPHER

Lesiba screamed when he woke from his nightmare. As wakefulness took possession of him, he was struck by three things: the sour taste in his mouth, the meowing of his neighbour's cat and the recollection of the dream. It was the third time in five years that he'd had the same dream. Each time, he would see himself wading through a snake-infested pit. There was this one green and blue snake that would strike his heel. And his attempts at bashing its head were always unsuccessful. He was not over-concerned by the bad omen; rather, he was irritated by the fact that it retarded the completion of his Book of Dreams – a diary in which he recorded all his dreams, past, present and future. He was already at Chapter One Hundred and Two.

Unlike previous times, when he had dismissed the dream, he started thinking of his potential enemies. Among his friends, Peter, Sonto, Mandla and Eddy, the last was the one who was starting to give signs of growing into a rival. They had in the past clashed over women. There were his work colleagues. Among them, Ketso, his departmental supervisor, was the one with potential for trouble. Though married, he was determined to frustrate Lesiba's chances of jolling with Benita. He knew, though, that Ketso was not a threat. The man was a lousy dresser, a lousy smoker who still stuck with BB Tobacco in the era of Peter Stuyvesant. He couldn't charm women or tell convincing lies. His only speciality was 'pimping' his subordinates to the bosses. It was common talk that Ketso's position was more of an affirmative-action gesture than a recognition of competency.

Outside Lesiba's door, lording over the whole township, there was Bra Shine, the ginsta with the perpetually clean-shaved scalp. Bra Morgan, the one with a panga scar running down the left side of his face. Both were rumoured to be members of one of the local Big Five gangs. Both drove colossal 'Be My Wife' BMWs. Though both were constantly associated with this or that crime, no life-valuing gossip-monger was foolish enough to sink his teeth into any of those rumours. Lesiba was one of the clever ones.

Jwalane was his common-law wife. She was a 'live-in' domestic maid in Craighhall Park and he saw very little of her. The few times she visited him in the township, she brought food parcels. Most of which, he was certain, had been 'self-donated' from the Madam's kitchen – wealth distribution on the smallest scale. He thanked his ancestors for such a considerate wife. It enabled him to spend his extra cash on luxuries like the horse races and regular church pilgrimages to different parts of the country. It was only when he missed her that he considered getting himself 'mmane-a-bana'. Those had their own problems: money or the other men they were involved with. He knew also that men of his times, like those of generations before, were brave and loving enough to kill over a woman – even if not to marry her, but to settle her with a dozen kids, and then spend the next ten years lamenting the lack of virgins to marry.

Jwalane... could he depend on her? Like men, most women were loving and caring – enough to spurn the advances of humble men besotted with them for the company of 'jackpots' like Bra Shine and Bra Morgan, who valued money. Not enough to work and earn it, but enough to kill for it.

He thanked his ancestors for their stinginess in not giving him some semblance of wealth. He was certain that Bra Shine and his bras would otherwise repossess it.

The dream of the snake-infested pit... that was not the only dream he dreamt. There were others. Dreams that would mount him and ride him to strange lands. Dreams that took him through streets paved with human flesh and bones. And there were times when bits of his own flesh would peel off to merge with the tar spread on the streets.

His reflections about the dream were disturbed by sounds of an AK-47 rifle. There was no need for panic, for he knew it was one of the local gangs engaged in target practice in preparation for yet another bank raid. With that comforting thought, he went back to sleep.

Arriving at work the following day, Lesiba found Ketso at his locker. On seeing him, Ketso hurried away. The previous night's dream came to mind, and Lesiba resolved to give the locker a thorough search later. He went looking for Mandla.

'Hey monna! What was old Kickso doing in my locker?'

'Scouting for love notes from Benita.'

'I'm serious, man. That ndala is up to something...'

'Kahle monna! He was probably after your scoff-tin.'

'I don't believe that. You know Kickso doesn't go vir jou smiley and runaways. He is 'n ou vir pizzas and buffet tables.'

It was one of the pair's lunch-time rituals to ridicule their supervisor.

Lesiba gave his locker thorough scrutiny. After patient searching, he found it: a copperish piece of tree bark. He wrapped it in a piece of A4 typing paper and took it home.

His dreams that night were erratic. He could not pin any of them down. He could see faces and figures, but they would lose their profiles the minute he tried to focus on them. The customary numbers that had helped him throughout the years to correctly bet the Chinaman and horses were also elusive that night. It was then that he regretted having taken Ketso's herb. Once more, the completion of his Book of Dreams was to be deferred because of a stupid error.

Three days later, he dreamt of himself having lost the ability to dream. That was not the only dream he dreamt. There were others as well…

Dreams that drew back their curtains before his eyes and screened gory pictures of his death in a car accident. Dreams that unveiled scenes of his hanging. At times it was punishment for the murder of his mistress's husband; at other times it was punishment for pick-pocketing infirm beggars.

The dream so shocked him that he resolved to go and consult an inyanga the following day. The man endowed with ancestral powers addressed him: 'Thank your ancestors for leading you to me in time. Had you wasted one more day, I tell you... your enemies are already sharpening their teeth to feast at your funeral.'

'There is a man... uyavuma? A tall, dark-complexioned man... uyavuma? There is a woman. Sometimes she steals your gourd and drinks from your stream. But I see her stealing from the streams of other men as well. Avoid her, her mouth is cursed and contaminated with the saliva of wild animals... uyavuma? There is a big tree... the tall dark man sometimes hides behind its trunk, sometimes he climbs it. His shadow always hangs about you. He absorbs all the sun-rays meant for you... uyavuma? I also see pages written, many lines of parables. The parables float around you.

Mostly you grab them, but of late they drift far and far away... Angry shadows hover around you. They want your parables...'

When the consultation ended, Lesiba was dazed. Arriving late at work, he told a lie – that his taxi had been involved in an accident. He noticed that everybody looked at him in a queer way. All were distant and aloof. Whenever he approached any of his colleagues, they dispersed.

The incident prompted him to amend the title of his book to the Book of Dreams and Parables.

That night, he again dreamt of the snake pit. He could distinctly see the other snakes. They all had human faces: his colleagues, neighbours and relatives. This time, though, he was able to make additions to his Book of Dreams.

The dream that would lead to his social ruin followed. It was a couple of weeks before the period of political turmoil in 1984. He titled it Dream Number Ninety-Seven, as it was his custom to title them numerically. In his dream, he saw black smoke descending over Alexandra. Men and women were choking and vomiting before falling to die in the alleys and gutters. An angel came and lifted him up above the smoke.

He made the terrible mistake of telling this dream to his priest during confession. He could tell the priest didn't like it by his frown. Much later, he was called by the Archbishop to clarify the matter. He was instructed never to tell other church members the dream, and to renounce the part about the angel as blasphemy. He was therefore surprised, days later, to see the Archbishop address a press conference. He told of the tragedy that would befall Alexandra.

Ten days later, the insurrection erupted. The Archbishop was hailed as a latter-day Nostradamus. Journalists besieged his house and the church. More converts joined. Lesiba secretly hoped to be promoted to the position of elder, but that never came. Instead, he was ostracised and accused of aspirations to usurp the Archbishop's position.

After that episode, he learned to keep his dreams to himself. He resolved to keep the book a secret. He spent sleepless nights consuming ink and paper, revising and recording the dreams. After recording sessions lasting weeks, he would go out gallivanting. It wasn't long before he awakened to the costs of that revelry. He would temporarily lose the power to retain or recall his dreams. This worried him a lot.

He consulted one of the church elders.

'Your ancestors are angry. They are taking what they gave. Worse will follow. Stop your gluttony, stop your gallivanting,' the elder cautioned.

Lesiba pondered these instructions. Finally, he concluded that it was better to sacrifice the pleasures of life – not out of desperation to finish the book or longing for the possible fame it might bring him, but because he knew that feeding some of the church elders with his prophecies was advancing his aspirations to the position of Archbishop, and the power and money that involved.

He was nonetheless haunted by worries that he had not as yet dreamt the ultimate dream. The dream that would reveal his destiny. He started fasting. On the third night of his fasting, the late Archbishop of Mount Galilee Christ Over the Cross Church in Zion appeared to him. He instructed Lesiba to part with Jwalane and devote his life to spreading the gospel.

Lesiba spend days brooding over these instructions, and finally sent Jwalane a letter:

Dear Jwalane

A couple of nights ago, a strange dream came to me. You are aware of my many previous dreams. Like the time I dreamt your mother was bitten by a crab. You will recall that, days later, she suffered a paralysing stroke. I constantly pray, Jwalane, that the dreams remain just that, but unfortunately they don't. Terrible happenings have followed after each.

My church elders have warned that unless I heed and obey this latest dream, my days in this world are numbered. Our late Archbishop, Baba Mandevu, has instructed me to forsake all earthly possessions and devote my remaining days to gathering his scattered sheep before the Seven Angels of Destruction descend on the earth.

Baba Nhlapho constantly preaches in church that Russia and America possess strange birds above the clouds that will converge on earth to announce Armageddon with terrible fires. He says all the waters from the world's seas will never put out those fires.

My wife, Jwalane, I know that by obeying Baba's instructions, I will be saving not only myself, but you and the Lord's many many children. As a devout Christian, I know you will understand. Until we meet again in the Lord's Ark.

I pray and wish you the Lord's blessings and forgiveness for all your sins.

Your devoted brother in the Lord
Lesiba

After hearing about the letter, Jwalane's parents called an urgent family kgotla. 'Take the fool for a good sjambokking at a people's court!' Jwalane's brother shouted.

'Kahle… that is not our custom. Call him and his parents to resolve the matter,' Jwalane's aunty countered.

'I tell you, he is sick. With those nonsense dreams. I heard he's after the Archbishop's chair.'

'Why not start his own little sect? Pretoria doesn't even bother registering them.'

'You all call him and resolve it, or I'll sort him. Nobody plays around with a sister of mine.'

Meanwhile, Lesiba's life continued. The frequency of his strange dreams increased. Those were not the only dreams he dreamt. There were others as well…

Dreams that used to blind his eyes with the inferno stoked at the holiest shrines. Dreams that would part like the Red Sea during Moses's exodus from Egypt and surrender his enemies to the torrid waves. There were also dreams of necklace victims. They would emerge riding on chariots, brandishing Eiffel Tower-sized torches, charging after their executioners.

Sometimes he would dream during the day. That was when he would engage in trying to interpret the dreams. He would close his eyes and see crowds of devotees prostrate before him, offering their reverence for the salvation he brought them. He started nurturing that dream into a probability; with time it matured into a reality. Except that reality occurred to him alone.

When the late Archbishop appeared again, he impressed upon Lesiba the need to double up the tempo of spreading the gospel. He stressed that the end was around the corner, 'and the Lord's Ark has only a driblet. Look at your sagging belly! I instructed you to forfeit earthly pursuits, yet you continue stuffing yourself.'

'But how will I survive? I don't know the difference between fasting and starving.'

'The One who commands will provide.'

Yes, he recalled that the One referred to did provide for John the Baptist in the desert.

The following day, Lesiba sent a message to Mandla to collect all the belongings from his locker and bring them to him.

Ketso relished the whole turn of events. When word spread around the factory that Lesiba had left work, he went about boasting, 'Who does he think he is? He is only a sick fanatic. I tell you, no stupid prayers can withstand my muti.'

Lesiba devoted his time to prayers and the interpretation of dreams. Multitudes started arriving to have their dreams interpreted. Some pleaded with him: 'Please, give me muti so that I can dream.'

'I am scared of my recent dream. Every time I dream about being run over by a bus packed with tourists.'

'Let us listen to the giver of dreams.'

Lesiba would always say: 'Let us ask the One who gives dreams to interpret them.' They then would bow their heads while he communicated with his God. At times it would happen quickly, while at other times he would be forced to remain bowed for close to an hour. Then, after another moment's meditative silence, Lesiba might say: 'I see you crossing mountains and rivers. Going to places where none of your people has ever been before.'

'Oh! Please, make it happen. I love to travel.'

Multitudes of young men and women started sniffing each other's heels as they raced to his house. Sometimes he would muffle a chuckle during these consultations. The young men mostly asked for help in being brought into contact with this or that virgin whom they claimed to have seen in their dreams. Some lamented the failure of their prayers: 'For six months, I have being praying to meet and marry Miss Alexandra. In my dreams it happens, yet all my efforts to meet her have failed.'

'The woman I constantly dream of making love to tells me I'm not her type when I propose to her.'

The young women also came in their droves.

'The man I love has a wife and two children. I have been praying for their death; it is now almost a year. Instead, the wife is getting fatter.'

'None of the fathers of my five children wants to marry me.'

To these, Lesiba would say: 'Be patient. The giver of dreams will unveil them when He is ready.'

Widows would come. They asked him to pray for them so that they would meet new husbands. Some would even confess to him that it was revealed to them in dreams that he was the man they should get married to. Among them were beautiful ones, and he would feel tempted. Not long after that, he started having the same strange dream for three consecutive weeks.

He tried to shut off the dream, dampen it with singing hymns and chants, but it refused to be expunged from his mind. The arrival of more widows, younger and more beautiful than previously, started interfering with his telepathic frequency. Meanwhile, the strange dream continued. He recorded it in his book as Dream Number One Hundred and Twenty-eight, and subtitled it: The Dream of a Dozen Orgies.

In the dream, I saw twelve men and women emerge from the Jukskei River. Their hands turned into knives and forks. They ran about sharpening these on rocks, brick walls and concrete pavements. They then turned and started chasing after each other. They sliced off each others' sex organs and roasted them on rocks along the river bank. They indulged in frenzied dancing and feasting. They ululated, while others started wailing, ranting and scratching their bodies. They poured the blood into wine glasses and offered toasts to each other.

Women suffered double, for once they had sliced off men's dangling members, they were left with nothing else. The men, however, came back running to slice off their remaining breasts.

> *The well-nourished, full-bellied men cut the left-over breasts into thin strands which they dried in the sun to make biltong. They then held a contest to see who had the largest store of biltong.*
>
> *A chanting Jwalane appeared. She ran brandishing a panga, determined to slice off my penis. Divine clemency prevailed, and I managed to break free from my trance before she could accomplish her mission.*

This dream shocked Lesiba. He could not reconcile it with the reality he so wished for. He wondered whether the dream had any telepathic link to his latest legion of followers, the widows.

This was not the only dream he dreamt. There were others as well...

Dreams that ripped the lids off coffins, tombstones off graves to reveal marytrs. Dreams of the blood of all murder and violent death victims, from Abel to those of modern carnages, gelling into giant waves and clouds that flooded the land, drowning all living organisms on earth. Dreams of aborted foetuses sealing closed the fallopian tubes of females universally. Dreams of harsh martial law and executions to counter the international solidarity and protest marches of redundant gynaecologists.

Mmadieketse, better known throughout the township as 'Cinzano Widow' or 'Ousie Deli', joined Lesiba's followers later. She was a strikingly beautiful twenty-seven-year-old. It was rumoured that her late bank robber boyfriend had left her a fortune: a shebeen in East Bank, a tavern in Selection Park, a ten-roomed double-storey mansion in Mmabatho and three cars: a 7-Series, a s'lahla and a dolphin. Of course, Lesiba was not attracted by her material status. He heard that she was haunted by a curse of losing all her men. They were snatched from her by either a knife or a bullet. He also wasn't interested in another rumour – that at the age of fourteen, she'd sold the life of her first boyfriend for a bottle of Cinzano. Others countered that it was Aurora whiskey.

'It is sheer luck that none of them has shown her his true colours. But I tell you, she'll meet her match one of these days.'

'Yaa! She double-crosses them against each other. Once they take hikes six-feet, she inherits their loot.'

'Who, Deli? Ka papa-ntsetse! That flat belly of hers is stuffed with jackrollers. Wait until they start coming out. The whole of Alex will be swarming with them. All these fancy privately owned cars will be repossessed by Deli & Sons Incorporated.'

Deli was loathed by women. Maybe it was just natural – very few of them could match her magnetic charms, or her talent at hitting 'jackpots'. But wasn't the Son of Man despised?

One night she came to see him. He prayed fervently for her: 'Lord, give me strength to guide this soul to salvation. Your stray lamb seeks Your embrace.'

'Baba, I am frightened. A Zionist prophet has warned that I will be knifed to death within days unless I repent. Please, Baba, pray for me.'

'Talk to the One above, His ears are sanctuary for wandering voices.'

'All the men I have planned to marry have passed away. The last one was shot two weeks ago.'

'To the One above let us turn. His generous ears are always there to offer refuge to wearied words. Let us pray for your soul, his soul and the souls of all the departed.'

As the two bowed their heads, Lesiba was aware of Deli's perfume. He was also aware that their heads were touching. In contrast to his audible praying, he could only hear her whispered murmur. It was then that he became aware of the minty fragrance drifting from her mouth.

'Baba, is it true…?' she suddenly whispered.
'Shhh! Pray, my child.'
'Is it true what they say, Baba?'
'What?'
'That since I didn't observe amasiko wethu after the death of my first boyfriend, all men who sleep with me will die.'
'You undoubtedly have sinned, my child. But remember the One above forgives seventy-seven times seventy-seven.'

Lesiba's prayer rhythm was disturbed. He stopped. He raised his face to find her looking at him appealingly. The deeper he looked into her eyes, the further and further away into oblivion he saw the desperate lost soul drift. He reached his hands out to save it from getting sucked into the abyss. 'Open your heart and soul to Him. Pray, my child. Remember He forgives seventy-seven times seventy-seven…'

At those comforting words, she collapsed into his arms. Hopeless, fragile body, already resigned to spiritual widowhood at twenty-seven. As her feminine body brushed against his, he felt a reversal of roles: he in the role of Mary, and she the baby Christ in his tender embrace.

When he woke up, it was one in the morning. Ousie Deli was snoring softly by his side. He slowly got off the bed and knelt by the door to perform his prayers of absolution. When he came back to bed, she was awake.

'I must go, Baba.'

'The world has grown teeth... I cannot allow you to venture out.'

'I am okay, Baba. I feel cleansed. I know nothing will harm me.' She kissed him before jumping off the bed and preparing to leave. He rubbed his eyes repeatedly, for he saw what appeared to be devilish silhouettes hovering around her. They were making obscene, threatening gestures at him.

A heavy pall wrapped around him. He shrugged his head to chase away sleep, but like a sedated patient on the operating table, he drifted back into slumber. He was in the depths of the pall when the late Baba Mandevu appeared.

'Heed! Adulterer, fornicator, where is my flock?'

'Baba, why do you frown on your devoted servant?'

'Go, sinner! You could not resist for one single night the temptations of earthly pleasures. Where have you led my lamb? Into the jaws of marauding wolves. With whom will I trust my flock, when my appointed shepherds turn to wolves?'

Lesiba tried to plead his case, but the Archbishop remained unrelenting.

'I have given you your dreams as your reward for leading my flock. All that you scorn to appease your lust.'

Lesiba tried harder to plead for forgiveness for his moral lapse. The late Archbishop remained steadfast in disclaiming him. He then instructed Lesiba to burn the manuscript of Dreams and Parables.

Lesiba woke up and sat on the bed. He could feel the rain lashing the roof. His blankets were warm and comforting. He found the idea of destroying his valuable book unacceptable and unappetising. He concluded that the late elder had confused his commands. Maybe he meant to instruct him to destroy all the newspapers and other books and magazines he read. With that comforting thought, he went back to sleep.

Much later, he was woken by the shattering of one of his windows. Vibrations of thunder followed. He turned to find the window bars mangled. The smell of burning paper drew his attention to the sideboard, where he kept the manuscript of his Book of Dreams and Parables. He saw only black, charred crisps of what used to be his valuable pages of concrete proof that dreams are part of reality. He could not decipher his delicate handwriting in that soot.

EPILOGUE

MY DUNGEON

from this side of the abyss
i constantly revisit the living
my hoarse voice takes flight
on drifting winds
to gather ears to warm its chilliness

i am wearied of wrestling
with the sun

yesterday a cat sneezed
at my strangeness
today my infant niece gave up
initiating me into the ways of life
spirits of laughter and smiles
flirt beyond my reach

from this side of the abyss
i re-enter my asylum
where darkness and my fury finds
patronage
boldly i will re-emerge
for a last heroic stance
an escape from myself.

OTHER FICTION TITLES BY JACANA

Ice in the Lungs
Gerald Kraak

The Silent Minaret
Ishtiyaq Shukri

Song of the Atman
Ronnie Govender

Uselessly
Aryan Kaganof

How We Buried Puso
Morabo Morojele

Kitchen Casualties
Willemien de Villiers

In Tangier We Killed the Blue Parrot
Barbara Adair

The Track
Katy Bauer

The Dreamcloth
Joanne Fedler

Bitches' Brew
Fred Khumalo